SAVING BIGFOOT VALLEY

SAVING BIGFOOT VALLEY

Published by Chapman Brown Books

ISBN-13: 978-1494364137
ISBN-10:1494364131

SAVING BIGFOOT VALLEY

SPIKE BROWN

Chapman Brown Books

DEDICATION

For Lyle, who took me to Willow Creek again and again.

1: Afternoon

THE valley was as exciting as watching worm snot drip off a blade of grass, thought Arrth. Especially when you were the only little Bigfoot. He stuffed another acorn in his mouth. That made ninety-nine. Five more, and he'd beat Taahmic's record. Too bad his friend wasn't there to see this. Or how different he looked now that his fur had turned a dark redwood brown.

He needed more nuts.

Just up the hill he spotted six gray squirrels zipping around the limbs of a huge old oak. It must be loaded with acorns. He raced to the tree. Five squirrels squeaked off, but one scurried to the top. It chattered angrily as Arrth grabbed a limb and swung himself up onto a sturdy branch. He hugged the trunk and shook. Leaves quivered. Limbs swayed. Nuts pelted into the carpet of dry grass underneath. He hopped down and gathered a handful.

"Five," he said and poked another nut into his already bulging cheeks. "Four. Three. Two."

"Arrth. Better not let your mother catch you sneaking snacks," said his father's voice.

Arrth jumped, spun round, and slipped on a patch of dried leaves. He landed with an "umph." In spite of his clenched jaws, a volley of nuts shot from his lips.

They pinged off rocks.

Bounced off tree trunks.

Flew into huckleberry thickets.

Thwacked his father's knees.

His father's eyes morphed to an annoyed smoke gray. He rubbed his right knee and frowned. "Arrth!"

That's when Arrth saw the blood. The light brown fur on his father's knee had turned a dark red. He felt his own eyes morph a nervous green.

"Sorry," Arrth said and spit out a dozen acorns. He swallowed a dozen more. "It was an accident."

"I know, but I'm afraid the Clan is getting tired of your little accidents. I can't keep making excuses. You're not a cub anymore."

Arrth looked at a dried oak leaf stuck between his furry toes.

"Firrth came to see me this morning."

Arrth let out a blast of air and smiled. He hadn't been near the old pond for days. That meant Firrth couldn't blame anything on him this time.

"What did he want?" Arrth asked.

"He said someone has been breaking the tops of the redwoods near the stream."

"Oh."

"You haven't been tree flying again, have you?"

"Who, me?" he said, thinking may rotten slime drop on the old tattle-tale's head.

"This has to stop."

"It doesn't really hurt the trees."

"Look around." His father pointed to a tall old redwood with a dead top. "See that tree? It's dying. Redwoods die from the top down. Snapping off their tops isn't good for them."

"They don't always break. Just sometimes."

"One time is one time too many." His father patted Arrth's shoulder. "I know you're bored and there's no one close to your age, but you can't keep climbing into treetops hoping they'll bend and then fling you into the air so you can fly. You're just too big."

"I wish Taahmic would come back." Arrth bit his lip and shrunk down, expecting his dad to explode. He'd been forbidden to talk about Taahmic, but five years was a long time to be friendless.

"Arrth." His father's voice carried a stern warning. "Remember, son, we are the keepers of the woods. One day you will take my place as The Chai. Now run along and don't get into any more mischief."

Arrth watched his father until he disappeared from sight and then took off at a dead run. Five minutes later and totally winded, he stopped and looked around. Snarfing weirdness. This part of the forest looked completely unfamiliar. He didn't recognize one tree, bush or fern. Hmmmm. He thought he and Taahmic had explored every inch of Bigfoot Valley.

He snagged a dead branch and drop kicked it with his big hairy foot. The limb somersaulted in the air until it came to a sudden stop.

That's when Arrth realized that his runburst had brought him close to the barrier that concealed his clan's existence from the primitive world outside the cloaked holo-shield.

This area was officially off limits, which made it all the more interesting. And exciting. Still, he didn't see why he'd been warned that it was dangerous. Trees looked the same. Moss still grew on the north side. Maybe the ferns were a little taller, but that didn't make them menacing. The only risk was if an adult spotted him. He'd be caved for a month.

He grinned. But that was only if he got caught.

Going into stealth mode, he crept close enough to touch the cloaked barrier. It was a one-way view. He could see out, but to anyone on the outside, the path looked like an unstable rocky cliff jutting skyward.

At least, that's the kind of thing he'd been told.

A branch snapped.

His brown eyes darted right and tingles zig-zagged from his

toes to his ears. He blinked. Unbelievable. Just the other side of the invisible barrier stood a creature with its back to him. Instead of fur, it wore a cloth hide colored with brown, green, and black spots. Even on its head. And it carried a metal stick.

"A skin-face!" he whispered.

2: Afternoon

ARRTH stared at the cloth-covered creature through the cloaked holo-shield. This was the first skin-monster he'd ever seen and it was not at all like he'd imagined. Ugly? Yes. But scary? Not really.

He sniffed, trying to catch its scent. Strange. From the stories he'd heard, he thought they all reeked like dead salmon after they spawned. This one didn't. It smelled like the peppermint that grew near the meadow.

The skin-face swung the metal stick it had been carrying up to its shoulder.

Arrth's fur bristled when he realized it was one of the killing sticks he'd been warned about by his father. The monster aimed at a jackrabbit. It had frozen in its tracks. Arrth had to do something. Now! Before it was too late!

He pushed against the cloaking shield and felt its sting run from the tips of his ears to the soles of his feet. The tingling pain didn't stop him. It only made him push harder and in seconds he'd burst through. Wow, he thought, and raced toward the hunter. If the shield was that easy to breach, how did the force field keep the skin-creatures out?

He slammed into the hunter.

The gun blasted.

A whistle of hot air ripped across his arm. He roared.

The skin-face screamed.

The jackrabbit came to life and bolted.

Arrth shoved the monster. It grabbed fur. They landed in a tumbled heap, grunting and growling as they rolled in the dirt. First one on top -- then the other.

Fists swung.

Feet kicked.

Elbows dug.

Knees rammed.

Each tried to punch the other's face, but missed. More shoving. More pushing. More rolling. Arrth landed a blow to the creature's stomach, and for a moment it stopped struggling.

Jumping to his feet, a sudden sharp pain dug into his ankle. He looked down. The skin-face had its arm wrapped around his leg and its teeth were buried in ankle fur.

Gross. The monster was biting him! What if it had rabies?

He shook his leg free, spun round, and ran back to the invisible wall. Using both hands he pushed against it. Nothing happened. It felt stronger from the outside, like a rock. A gunshot exploded the bark of a tree to his right.

He dropped flat on his belly, landing with his nose just inches from an unusual granite boulder with dark red spots.

He glanced back. The skin-face had the long gun pointed at him.

He scrambled to his feet and in one swift movement grabbed the spotted boulder and hurled it at the monster. Then he bent low and rammed into the barrier with his shoulder. The invisible wall shuddered and he broke through. Not daring to look back, he ran, zig-zagging this way and that.

Soon the only sounds he heard were the thuds of his pounding feet and his own gasps. Still, he didn't stop until he reached the creek a good mile inside the barrier.

His tongue felt like dead moss. He dropped to his knees, bent to drink the clean sweet water and went slack-jawed. Reflected on the water's flat surface was a skin-face with bright green eyes and big flat teeth. What? Had it followed him? No, that wasn't possible. Then how had it got inside? He leaped to his feet and rotated in the air with his fists clenched.

Where was the skin-face?

It couldn't have just disappeared. Everyone knew they were slow like slugs. It must be hiding. Arrth searched under bushes and behind rocks.

No skin-face.

He shimmied up a tree and scanned the forest floor.

Still, no skin-face.

He dropped down and rubbed his head. His eyes almost popped onto the ground.

A huge wad of brown fur filled his hand. His fur. He looked back into the water. The eyes of the skin-face were now a bright sky blue. He moved right. It moved with him. He blinked. It blinked. He licked his lips. It licked its lips. He touched his face and watched the beast in the pool touch its cheek.

Arrth's stomach lurched. It was his face, his eyes blue from fright. What had happened to his fur?

Had the creature's bite turned him into a skin-face?

No. This couldn't be happening. Not to him. What was he going to do? He couldn't let anyone see him like this.

He scooped mud from the bank and smeared it on his forehead and then on his chin and cheeks. It worked, sort of. At least he didn't look like a monster anymore. He sighed and saw his eyes morph from blue to a pale brown.

He picked up a rotten log and dashed it into the water-mirror. It splattered into wild circles. Cool water splashed his thigh. Tiny trickles raced down his fur and onto another patch of bare skin at his knee.

"Noooooooooo," he moaned.

More skin. More mud. More loose fur.

In the end he looked like a giant walking mud ball.

He let out a wild cry. Startled birds shot from trees. Lizards awoke and darted under rocks. Beavers abandoned logs and slipped into the stream.

Why had he had touched that disgusting skin-face?

Why?

He had to get home before it got worse. His father would know what to do. That is, if he didn't kill Arrth first for breaking Bigfoot Law.

3: Late Afternoon

ARRTH raced toward his home, avoiding the main paths.

He slid down rocky slopes, jumped over fallen logs, and dodged low-hanging limbs. Almost there, he hid in a thicket of blue-flowering tick brush to catch his breath and studied the entrance into the narrow cave canyon.

His skin itched, but he was afraid to scratch. Afraid he'd lose more fur.

Good. At least no one hustled along, coming or going on the winding paths that led to the pod caves. No one sat on a porch soaking up sunrays. Of course this didn't mean they weren't inside looking out through a private cloaking door.

From here he'd have to bush whack through the dense brush, go up and over the hill, and come in from above. At least his family cave rested on the highest level with only a fifty-foot drop down to its porch.

He scrambled up the hill and struggled through a patch of clinging Himalayan berries. At the top he paused to catch his breath. The clouds overhead swirled like a giant sky whirlpool. Below, he scanned the twin trails snaking down both sides of the cave canyon walls.

No one was out and about.

He swung down, dropped onto the porch, and hurried into his family cave, which was dimly lit by phosphorescent lichen. His eyes adjusted to the lower light. What snarking luck. No one was home. He darted into his personal pod. Instantly the fireflies awoke. They swarmed to the ceiling, lighting the room. The flies had been a gift from his grandfather for Arrth's seventy-fifth birthday, all the way from Kansas.

He paused, afraid to face his reflection in the polished rock mirror. At the same time he had to look. He opened one eye. Not good. The mud on his skin had dried in patches. Some places it had cracked and had flaked off, showing pink skin. Bare scratched skin that itched. He sniffed the ugly red streak on his upper arm where the long gun's bullet had stung him.

His eyes speed-morphed from green, to blue, to brown. He was so dead.

Rattles slid over his foot. He reached down and picked up the little snake.

"Oh Rattles, what am I going to do? I'm turning into a skin-face."

The snake gave what sounded like a sympathetic hiss.

Arrth rubbed its head. "What am I going to tell Dad? He's going to kill me."

Rattles' tongue flicked bare skin on Arrth's ear.

"Hey, that tickles." He set Rattles on top of his treasure trunk. "But if I don't tell Dad what happened, how will he know how to fix things?"

Rattles coiled into a circle, tucked its rattles under its head, and stared at Arrth.

"Okay, I'll tell him. Everything."

He rubbed the mud off the bite on his ankle. Snarfing weirdness. There was nothing there. Not even teeth marks.

"Wait! What if my fur loss has nothing to do with the skin-face? It must be because I went through the barrier without turning it off." He grinned. "Dad will know how to reverse those effects. If not, Uulmer will." He laughed. "Which means I don't have to tell him about the skin-face."

He hopped and punched the air.

"I'll only be in half the trouble."

A loud howl interrupted his celebration.

His mother. Her roar grew louder, and she did not sound happy. "I just polished this floor! Who tracked in all this mud? Their furry feet are in big trouble. Arrth!"

The floor vibrated as she stomped into his pod.

He tried to hide behind the treasure trunk. Rattles slithered under it.

"Arrth! You can't hide from me. Do you have any idea how hard I work to keep this place nice?"

He crouched lower. "Sorry, Mom," he mumbled.

"Sorry's not good enough. You'll clean every inch of the floor and then maybe you'll have less trouble remembering to wipe your feet. Now come out from behind there and face me when I'm talking to you."

He bit his lip, stood, and stared at the floor. If she was this upset about the mud, what would she do when she realized he'd been outside? That his fur had fallen out and that he could be dying. Would she care about that as much as she cared about her clean floor?

She snorted. When she spoke her voice came out high-pitched and squeaky. "Look at me."

He raised his head and squeezed his eyes shut. He didn't want her to see them morphing.

"What are you trying to hide? Why are your eyes closed?"

He opened one eye, expecting to see her fiercest glare. Instead, she grinned from ear-to-ear. Her hand covered over her mouth, but it didn't hide the huge smile that peeked out from both sides of her hairy fingers. A strange bubbling sound rumbled in her throat.

When he realized she was laughing, he shouted, "It's not funny."

"But you're so cute," she cooed. "Reminds me of when you were a cub. I can't wait until your father gets home."

"You think I'm cute. Don't you care that I might be dying?"

She laughed. "You're not dying, my sweet little Bigfoot cub. It's just a phase."

"Losing fur is a phase?"

She nodded. "A right-of-passage. All little Bigfoots go through it, but I'll let your father explain when he gets home. Boy will he be surprised you're such an early bloomer. You're only seventy-seven. We didn't expect your transition for another four or five years."

And explain his father did . . . in more than Arrth wanted to hear.

4: Night

ARRTH lay flat on his stomach behind a veil of variegated ivy. His mother had planted it to hide the old-fashioned carved shelf over his pod door. She said the indoor greenery looked modern. His father had rolled his eyes but had said nothing. Arrth knew what that meant and usually he agreed with his dad. Not this time. He liked the screened shelf. It became his favorite hiding place with its perfect view of the main cave.

Rattles silently slithered up the wall and onto the shelf.

Arrth ignored the little snake as it draped around his neck. He was too busy watching and listening.

His mother paced the floor. His father sat at his info-communicator, scrolling through Bigfoot News. Arrth knew they thought he was asleep, but how could he sleep? He'd just found out that he'd be bald for six months. That is, except for his eyebrows and eyelashes, because they were already hair and not pup fur. It was the fur you shed. What grew back would be his adult hair.

On top of that, there were all sorts of DO'S and DON'TS.

The big DON'T: don't eat apples because apple seeds contained chemicals called cyanogenic acids, whatever they were. These acids affected some follicle gland during the transition. If he ate even one bite of apple it might retard the growth of his adult hair. Permanently. Plus, you'd grow old fast like the skin-faces did.

He shivered. How horrible, looking like a skin monster for the rest of a short life. He vowed not to eat any apples until he was done with the transition thing.

Still, why couldn't the banned food have been celery roots or watercress?

A useless questions. His transition had its own season. His dad had made that part perfectly clear.

Other parts weren't so clear, and he sensed his father had held something back. Something more important than fur loss or his voice changing. That's why Arrth lay behind the vines spying on his parents. It was the only way to find out what was really going on.

Rattles' tongue flicked his ear.

"Cut it out," he whispered. 'You're going to get us caught." He pulled the snake from his neck.

His mother stopped pacing. "We're not going to let him do it," she said. "It's too dangerous."

His father sighed loud enough to wake the sand mites. "It's not dangerous. It's tradition."

"Then it's time to change tradition. We can't let Arrth do it. Not after what happened to Taahmic."

Taahmic?

Arrth cocked his head to the side and leaned forward. Was he finally going to find out what had happened to his best friend? Five years earlier Taahmic had disappeared. It happened while Arrth vacationed with his grandfather in the tall mountains. When he came back, no one would talk about it.

At least not to Arrth, but that didn't stop him from asking. He questioned everyone until he'd become a pest.

"No more questions," his father had ordered. "No more talk of Taahmic."

Arrth stopped asking, but he hadn't forgotten his old friend.

"Worm meat!" roared his father.

The polished crystal info-screen filled with red and green wavy lines. "This is the second time tonight. Something's wrong with the power."

"Have you been listening to me?" Arrth's mother asked.

His father clicked off the fuzzy screen, stood, and cracked his knuckles. "Yes, dear. I have. The whole mess was an unfortunate accident."

"Accident? Are you calling what happened to Taahmic an

accident?"

"Enough. You're worried about nothing. It happened once. It won't happen to our son."

"That's because he's not doing it. He's too young and the risk is too great. He can do something safe. You could take him to the ocean to swim with the sharks. Or let him jump off a cliff. Anything other than giving him a *Night Out*."

A night out, that was dangerous? More like boring. His parents regularly went on night outs for dinner, old-old music, and dancing. Tonight, his spying had turned out to be a total snarfing waste.

"You know it's more than just tradition," his father said. "Don't you remember your first night out?"

Arrth's right leg seized up in a cramp, all the way from his big toe to his waist.

He shifted positions and accidently bumped Rattles. The snake slid off the shelf. His hand shot out to catch his pet. Instead, he snagged his mother's precious ivy. He started to fall and grabbed at another clump of vines. The green veil ripped from the wall.

He crash-landed onto the hard stone floor. He rolled onto his back and winced under his father's stern glare.

"Uhh, hi, Dad. Mom."

5: Late Night

ARRTH'S **father looked** like he was about to blast an acorn out both ears.

"Why aren't you in bed?" he said.

Arrth stared at his hairless toes. "I wanted to know what's going on. I heard you talking about me."

"It's nothing you need to worry about."

"Why didn't you tell me about my *Night Out*?"

"Because," his mother interrupted. "You're not doing it."

His father's dark grey eyes locked on his mother's in a silent staring match. It seemed to last forever. His parents rarely fought, but when they did . . . he'd strap on his vid screen and play Skin-face Slayer. By the time he'd smashed ten levels of skin-faces, it was usually safe to unplug.

"I'm the Bigfoot in this household," his father shouted. "I make the decisions." His thunderous voice shook the table and chairs.

Rattles slithered into Arrth's pod.

He wanted to follow. Run away, but then it'd be just like when Taahmic had disappeared; everyone else knowing except him. This time he wouldn't back down. Not until somebody explained the night out.

"You're not the only one with big feet in this cave. I'm his mother and I say he's not doing it."

Her black eyes flashed with red fire. Arrth's newfound nerve started to fade. What was he thinking? He should get out of there, before she turned her anger on him.

But . . . if he did . . .

No. Not this time. Somehow he dredged the courage to stay put. He gripped the back of his father's chair and said, "Will someone tell me what it is?"

"He has a right to know," his father said.

His mother humphed, spun around, and stomped into their room. The privacy shield snapped down. Seconds later the sound of a raging waterfall spilled from the pod.

Arrth couldn't believe it when his father raised his hands and gave her the angry double-clap. Whoa. Arrth's eyebrows shot up. That was worse than flicking a booger in a slammer fight.

His mother turned up the volume even louder and the floor throbbed. Wow. If Arrth cranked up his sound machine that loud, he'd be caved for a week.

His father tossed Arrth a blanket from the back of the couch and motioned for him to follow. They went out on the front porch and settled on a log bench. The dark cool air prickled his skin. Freaky. Talk about cold. How did the skin-faces stand it?

He pulled the blanket tighter.

He wanted to tell his father to get on with it, but he knew that if he did, it would have the opposite effect. So he stared into the night sky, waiting. The stars glittered like dew drops at first light. Six months would be a really, really long time to be furless. And cold. And shivering.

No wonder the skin-faces wore cloth.

He looked at his father, surprised at his huge smile.

"I can still see your mother when she returned from her *Night Out*. Running back into the valley. Her eyes shone bright like a pair of glittering June bugs. I fell in love with her that day."

"Dad," Arrth interrupted. "I don't want to hear all that mushy stuff. Just tell me about my night out."

His father blew a blast of air through his nostrils.

Arrth frowned and bit down on his lower lip hard. Why hadn't he kept his mouth shut?

His father took a deep breath and to Arrth's relief, continued.

"For centuries, the *Night Out* has been the time-honored test of transition from childhood to adulthood. How one handles it is the mark of one's measure."

"The mark of one's measure," Arrth repeated. "And the *Night Out* is?"

"It starts at home... There were five of us my year. Uulmer, Red Fur, Firrrth, and Moss."

Arrth rolled his eyes. When was his dad going to get to it? Before he could stop himself, he blurted out, "Is this part of the story necessary?"

His father smiled, showing his long eyeteeth. "It is if you want me to tell you about your upcoming *Night Out*."

"Okay." Arrth huddled in his blanket and tried not to sigh out loud.

"I stood at my front door, waiting for the signal. It seemed like forever before Mootak beat the sounding log; the ancient ceremonial call to step from the safety of the home cave. To symbolically leave childhood behind."

"Mootak? The same Mootak that lives on the first tier? I knew he was an old-old, but I didn't think he was that ancient. He must have at least seven hundred years!"

"Seven hundred and twenty-five. Now stop interrupting." His father tapped his fingers on the log. "Unless you'd rather go to bed."

"Sorry."

"Where was I?"

"There were five of you."

"Yes, five of us that year. After the last drum beat, we simultaneously stepped onto our respective porches. Everyone else gathered below on the canyon floor with torches, looking up at us. We waited until Mootak shouted, 'Go forth into the world!' and we took off. Our parents and friends whistled encouragement as we raced down, each of us hoping to be the first outside."

"You mean, outside of the barrier? They let you go out? Without an adult?"

"Yes."

"So, were you first?"

Brum, brum, brum, broke the silence and echoed up the canyon. Had talking about it summoned Mootak to beat the sounding log?

At the same moment the path lights blinked and faded to black.

His father jumped up. Porch lights flicked on, up and down the canyon. Cloaking doors popped open. Everyone, torches in hand, streamed from their caves. The flame balls bounced like monster-sized lighting bugs racing down the paths toward the forest.

"What is it?" Arrth asked.

His mother appeared at the door. "What's happened?"

"I don't know," his father said.

"Is it time for my night out?" Arrth asked and then realized, what a stupid question.

"No," his parents said in unison.

"Go to bed, Arrth," his father said. "We'll finish our talk in the morning."

6: Midnight

ARRTH **plunked down** on the carved bench by his cave door and ground his teeth until the back of his head hurt. Even if he was the youngest member of the clan, that didn't mean he should be left out of everything. Something important had happened tonight and instead of being treated like an almost-adult, he'd been ordered to bed.

Totally unfair. He wasn't a little cub who had to be protected from the big bad world. He'd proved that earlier when he'd saved the rabbit from the skin-faced hunter.

It was time for things to change. And tonight was the night.

He waited until the upper level pathways cleared. Sticking to the shadows, he scurried down the hand-hewn trail until he came up behind an old-old creeping along at a slug's pace. Just his luck. Meadowlark. She would take forever, humming her strange melodies as she made her way to the Emergency Meet.

Getting impatient wouldn't move her any faster, and even though she was half- crazy, he couldn't let her see him. He backed up the trail and leaned against a rock to wait her out. To pass time he'd count stars.

One, two . . . one thousand twenty-five.

Cool wind bristled his skin as shivers raced down his back. He tied two ends of his blanket round his neck and wrapped the rest of it around his body. That's when he felt something coil around his ankle. He jumped.

"Rattles! What are you doing here?"

He lifted the little snake to eye level. The snake's tongue flicked his nose.

"Okay, I know it's my fault. I left the door open, but you have to quit following me. You could get lost. Or someone could step on you."

Meadowlark's crooning voice drifted on the wind. "Rock-a-by Cubby, in the tree top. When the earth shakes, the branches will flop. When the earth slides, the tree trunk will break. And down will fall Cubby, to swim in the lake."

"I should take you home," Arrth said, "but it sounds like Meadowlark is almost down to the bottom."

He squinted at the sky and then blinked hard several times. Was something wrong with his eyes, too?

Overhead, the night's veil pulsed and stars shifted in and out of focus. Fuzzy undulating streaks shimmered like someone had spattered techno sap in the sky.

"What's wrong?" he whispered to Rattles. "This is snarfy weird. Come on, I'm taking you home. It's not safe for a little snake cub outside."

By the time he returned, Meadowlark had finally reached the bottom. On flat ground she moved a little faster. When she rounded the big fir tree, he slipped down the path and into the woods. He kept low and moved as quick as he could wearing a stupid blanket that kept snagging on things. He crept toward the gathering place. The excited hum of voices sounded like a beehive convention.

He slipped into a thicket of huckleberry brush. From there he had a clear view of the covered amphitheater carved into the rock cliff. Instead of the usual bright techno lights from above, blazing torches sprouted on tall poles strategically placed to light the area. Front and center, a bonfire blazed. The combined flames from the torches and fire cast a flickering yellow pall on the gathering.

The Bigfoot adults gathered in clumps, all talking at once and waving their arms. At least he hadn't missed anything. The Emergency Meeting hadn't started yet. He spotted his parents and his breath quickened. This was just like when he and Taahmic had played Bigfoot and Skin-face. They'd taken turns being the monster and stalked one another. When that got old, they stalked the adults. Eventually that got old, too.

One particularly boring day Taahmic had asked, "You know what would be really electrifying?"

"What?"

"To spy on real skin-faces. There's a skin-town near here. We could go, spy, and be back before anyone knew we were gone."

Of course they never went, but planning it was totally snarfy.

Sometimes Arrth still played the game. Like tonight. Hiding and spying on the adults. Only tonight he wasn't playing and this wasn't a game. Something seriously bad had happened if Mootak couldn't wait until daylight to call a meeting.

Meadowlark finally arrived.

Mootak nodded to her and moved to the hollow log-drum near the fire. She tottered to the nearest bench, sat, and leaned forward on her staff. Mootak beat a short rhythm on the log. Instantly everyone stopped talking and found seats. Arrth's parents sat near the top.

He wished he could see Mootak's face. Maybe he should back out of his present position, move to the right twenty feet, and sneak in close again. He grinned. It'd be easy. A piece of honeycomb. His spy skills were the snarfiest.

Arrth pulled the blanket over his head and inched backward.

Mootak began. "I've called you all here because we are on the brink of a catastrophe. The cloaking shield is faltering. In the last five hours we've had six power surges and three blackouts."

The crowd gasped. Arrth took advantage of the moment and dashed behind a tree.

"If it fails completely, we must be ready to evacuate."

"Leave our homes? That's crazy," shouted one female down front.

Several males leaped to their feet, all shouting at the same time. This was horrible.

Arrth used the chaos to slip from tree to tree. He needed to see Mootak's face. The old-old one raised his hands for silence.

"Please," he said. "One at a time."

"What's wrong with the device?" Red Fur, the tall Bigfoot sitting next to Arrth's father, shouted. "Can't it be fixed?"

"At this time we don't know what's wrong with it."

"Then get a new cloaking device!" someone shouted.

“That’s easier said than done. The tech that designed our system died last month and it’ll take at least a hundred years to duplicate his work. We don’t have a hundred years.”

“Why hasn’t it been fixed?”

“Uulmer’s run the usual diagnostic tests, but has come up with nothing. Until we know what’s wrong, it can’t be repaired.”

“Where’s Uulmer? Why isn’t he here?”

“As we speak, he’s running the perimeter, searching for any signs of damage.”

Damage? Arrth slumped against the rough bark of a tree. Had his unauthorized push through the cloaked perimeter wall made it quit working? Was this his fault?

“You must prepare yourselves. If the cloaking device fails, we can’t stay.” Mootak paused. “If the skin-faces see into our land, it will only be a matter of time before they come to hunt us.”

Arrth felt sick. What had he done? Why had he pushed through the barrier when he knew it was against Bigfoot Law?

“Look!” Red Fur shouted and pointed.

Arrth cringed, afraid to face his accuser. It was all over now.

7: Midnight Plus 1 Hour

EVERYONE seated in the amphitheater shifted positions. They all tried to see what Red Fur pointed to in the dark. The flickering light from the torches licked the cool air, the faint flutters challenging the night. Pop. Crackle. Snap. The bonfire sent a shower of cinders into the sky.

Arrth started to stand, his legs stiff from crouching for so long.

Why did Red Fur have to spot him? His life was ruined. He should just dig a deep hole and hibernate for the next hundred years. Maybe by then they'd forgive him for destroying the cloaking device.

"It's Uulmer," Red Fur shouted. "He's back."

The crowd erupted, shouting, whistling, and stamping their feet.

Uulmer burst into the light. "I know what's wrong with the cloaking shield," he shouted between gasps. "One of the perimeter devices is missing."

"What? What? What?" Everyone shouted at once. Even his father.

"What's happened to it?"

"How's that possible?"

"What do you mean, missing?"

So it wasn't Arrth's fault. Relieved, he moved up to a few feet behind Meadowlark seated on a log and used her for a shield. She'd never hear him. She was half-deaf.

Things might be terrible, but at least his spy skills were still snarfing hot.

Mootak raised his hands. "Silence."

Everyone sat, still muttering.

"If there is one more outburst, this meeting is over," Mootak scolded. "Acting like a bunch of ignorant skin-faces won't bring a solution to this grave situation. Be patient. Each of you will have the opportunity to speak." He held up one finger. "One at a time."

Arrth almost laughed out loud. Seeing the adults get in trouble was funny. Most looked at their feet and hummed apologies. Even his parents. For the first time he could imagine them young cubs.

Mootak cleared his throat. "Uulmer, which perimeter device is missing?"

"The one near the south ridge."

Arrth's mouth went dry. That's where the skin-face had bit him.

"And you're sure it's gone? You searched the entire area?" Mootak asked.

"Yes."

"No rock slides? Not covered by moss? Didn't roll down the hill?"

Uulmer shook his head to each question.

Mootak motioned with an open palm to the seated audience. "Not all of us are techno experts. Tell us how the perimeter devices work."

"There are twelve of them placed at twenty-mile intervals around our boundary. Each one communicates with its neighboring devices. Together, they create the chain of cloaking illusions necessary to keep out prying skin-eyes."

"Can't it work with eleven?"

"For a time, but not indefinitely. And, not perfectly. Look up. The morphing sky is a side-effect of the missing device. The power surges are another problem. They're disrupting our communication net and will increase. Without all the devices in place, the whole system will fail."

Mootak frowned. "How long do we have?"

"My guess is five days."

"Can we get a new one delivered?"

Ulmer shrugged. "Not in five days. Maybe never. The designer died. It could take a hundred years to duplicate his work."

Shouted rumbles rippled across the audience.

"There's more," Uulmer began, but Mootak silenced him with a wave.

"It's their turn to speak," Mootak said. "You can continue your lecture after they've had their say."

"But. . ."

"We'll start at the top left." Mootak said.

Red Fur stood. "So our evacuation is imminent?"

"Without the system, our existence will no longer be a skin-face legend," Mootak said.

The next female said, "Then we can't stay. The skin-faces will kill us."

"Or worse, put us in one of their zoos," another said.

Arrth's father stood next. "The system isn't down yet. Instead of hysterics, we should recover the device. They don't have legs. Someone took it and we have to get it back. What does it look like?"

Mootak nodded to Uulmer.

"It's about the size of a watermelon," Uulmer said, "and disguised to look like a piece of granite embedded with garnets. Nothing special or unique. Granite boulders cover the hillside. "

Arrth's eyes widened. His legs felt weak. Oh, no. That sounded like the rock he'd thrown at the skin-face. It was his fault the cloaking device was failing. One stupid mistake and he'd put the whole clan in danger.

This wasn't a game. It was real.

His father raised another question. "Were there signs that someone had been there?"

Uulmer nodded. "That's what I started to say earlier. I saw skin-face bootprints. The retreating prints left deeper impressions than the approaching ones. It could have been carrying the device. There were additional signs that the skin-face had used a long gun." He paused and then added, "One last thing. I also saw clan footprints. Small ones."

Arrth felt his stomach sink and his skin burned hot like a fever.

"Small footprints?" his father said.

Everyone stared at him.

"A cub's footprints," Uulmer said.

"There's only one kid in the valley," Red Fur said. "What was your son doing outside?"

Meadowlark sang, “You can ask him. He’s right behind me.” She turned and pointed to where Arrth hid.

8: Midnight Plus 2 Hours

ARRTH pulled the blanket over his head.

With a groan he stepped from the night's shadow into the naked torchlight. Even without looking, he could feel their stares. His parents'. Mootak's. Uulmer's.

"Arrth!" his father roared from the top level of the amphitheater.

Flinching, Arrth tried to shrink into his skin.

"What are you doing here?"

Arrth ground his teeth and hunched lower. At least the blanket hid the blaze of heat that exploded like an uncontrollable wildfire consuming his bare skin.

"When I get home, you'd better be in your bed. Asleep!"

"Wait," Mootak said, before Arrth had a chance obey his father. "It would be premature to send away the younger without learning what he knows."

His father's eyes locked on Mootak's in a silent, challenging stare. Then he shifted his gaze to his son.

Arrth stood frozen, afraid to even breath.

With a final shake of his head, his father grunted, and sat.

The old-old motioned for Arrth to move closer. "It is good the boy is here. I believe he has important answers. Come here."

The old-old touched his shoulder and the questions began.

"You saw the skin-face?"

"Yes." Arrth's voice was a whisper.

"Tell us about it."

Arrth stared at the old-old's knees and spoke so low only Mootak could hear. "It was ugly. All skin and covered in a spotted cloth hide."

"The boy says, the creature was ugly and covered in spotted cloth. Now speak up. If I have to repeat everything you say, we will still be here when the system goes down. Hurry up. Tell us everything. We haven't much time."

Arrth forced himself to speak louder. "I was out scouting . . ." His voice squeaked. His hand flew to his throat. What now?

He dry swallowed and started again. "I pretended to be a perimeter scout. That's when I saw it. The monster. It was going to kill a rabbit with a long gun. I had to go outside to save it."

Two of the topmost torches had burned to the nub. Wispy smoke trails trickled from them and dissipated into a murky haze.

"I didn't know the monster took the device. Why would he want a rock?"

"Is there anything else you haven't told us?"

"No. I don't think so." Nothing except it had bit him and that he'd thrown the rock at it.

Uulmer spoke up. "Whether we evacuate or not, we need to get that device back. It can't be left in skin-face hands. If they discover the science behind cloaking, no clan will be safe."

Chapter 9: Midnight Plus 3 Hours

ARRTH stomped toward the cave canyon, growling like an angry bear cub. His clenched fists swung forward and back, leaving the blanket to flap like a giant bat wing behind him.

"Spider spit! Slug slime! Worm snot!"

Why did Mootak have to send him home? None of the adults had seen the creature or knew what it looked like. He'd recognize it if he saw it again.

He frowned.

Okay, maybe it might look different if it changed its cloth hide. But even if it did, no one else could identify its unforgettable sweet peppermint scent.

"It's not snarking fair. I'm an almost-adult. I should be treated like one."

He stumbled on a rock in the path and kicked it. The apple-sized stone clattered down the trail and stopped. When he caught up to it, he kicked it again.

And again.

And again.

And again.

Each time harder, and each time it flew farther. By the time he'd reached Meadowlark's cave pod, he blamed her. If she hadn't ratted him out, he'd still be at the meeting. Not being sent home like a stupid little cubby.

He kicked the rock at her doorway.

Instead of bouncing off, it flew through, and ricocheted inside. Ping. Ping. Ping. Thud.

Meadowlark had forgotten to cloak her door.

He bit his lip, thinking that he hadn't been in Meadowlark's cave since Taahmic disappeared. Why would he? He had no interest in her old-old music sticks or listening to her ramble on and on about old boring stuff no one was interested in. Not even his father.

But . . . the thud of the rock bouncing off her cave wall had triggered forgotten memories. Memories of a wrestling match and of knocking one of her precious vision stones to the floor. Memories of eating honeyed nutmeats until his stomach hurt. Memories of the secret hidey-hole where Taahmic kept a stash of treasures he didn't want his grandmother to see. Treasures just sitting there. Waiting to be rediscovered.

Should he? Did he dare?

Arrth looked out over the darkened canyon. The black silhouette of an owl swooped into a tree and settled on a branch. Perched perfectly still, it began to call soft soothing hoots. "Hoo, hoo, hoo."

Were the hoots a sign?

No one else knew about the hidey-hole. Not even Meadowlark. Maybe Taahmic had left a clue in it for Arrth.

He bopped his head with the flat of his hand. He should have thought of that, years ago. Okay, that didn't matter. He'd thought of it now.

It was his duty to sniff out any and all clues to his best friend's disappearance. To find out the truth even if it was five years too late.

Besides, everyone was still at the meeting, except for Uulmer. But his techno cave was on the lower level on the opposite side of the canyon. There was no way he could see this far. Not in the dark.

Arrth slipped into the pitch-black cave. He felt his way to Taahmic's pod and had a terrifying thought. What if Meadowlark had discovered the hidey-hole? No, she couldn't have. It was too cleverly disguised.

Once he was inside Taahmic's old room, he shut the door and activated the lights. He squinted against the sudden light.

"Nooooo," he groaned. "Not snarking fair."

The room was empty. Not totally empty, but all of Taahmic's things were gone. In place of the bed, a stack of redwood stick-limbs waited for Meadowlark to record her songs. The huge pile blocked the hidey-hole.

Was there time to move them and put them back before

Meadowlark returned? He'd have to chance it.

He set to work. Grabbing an armful at a time, he started a new pile in the center of the pod. Hurry, hurry. Meadowlark could come back any second. Finally with the job done, he wiped his sweating palms on the blanket and admired the mural Taahmic had carved into the stone wall. Bigfoots. Hills. Mountains. Trees. Flowers. Deer. Birds. And skin-faces.

Why had Meadowlark covered it up? It looked amazing.

Arrth rapped on the wall with his knuckles until he heard a familiar hollow echo. He pushed on the big nose of the nearest skin-face and a segment of the wall popped open. Taahmic's treasures still rested in a neat pile. Pinecones. Pebbles. And a carving of a raccoon.

Boom. Boom. Boom.

The Meeting had ended. He grabbed Taahmic's vid-cube.

No time to move the pile of tree limbs back to their original position. Maybe Meadowlark wouldn't notice. But maybe she would. It didn't matter. He had to get out of there. It might take her a long time to walk back, but his parents weren't so slow.

He tucked the vid-cube under his arm, turned off the lights, and raced from the cave.

Voices drifted on the wind. Torches emerged from the woods and started up the paths on both sides of the canyon. He raced home and into his pod.

Rattles' tail vibrated as if to greet him.

"Shhhhhhhh."

He coiled the snake on the pillow, settled into his moss mattress, and clutched the vid-cube. Scrunching lower he pulled a spider-web blanket over his head.

Rattles tried to unwind.

"Stop it!" Arrth hissed. "You're going to get me into trouble. Now pretend you're asleep."

The main cave's cloaking door slid open.

10: Midnight Plus 4 Hours

ARRTH lay wide-eyed in his bed, clutching Taahmic's vid-cube under the covers. He was too excited to sleep, and too afraid to play the cube until his parents had fallen asleep.

It seemed like forever until their snore vibrations rattled his rock collection in his treasure chest. Once the pebbles began to rub and click together, he started counting. One, two . . . fifteen. . . twenty-five . . . forty-nine . . . one hundred . . . one hundred seventy-four . . . two hundred.

He eased out of bed and grabbed his earplug from his portable sound machine. He considered going outside, but decided it was safer to stay in his room. Sometimes his mom had supersonic hearing, even when she was sound asleep.

It would be a snarfing waste to have the cube confiscated before he had a chance to view it.

He slipped back into bed, plugged in the earphone, and turned on the cube. Nothing happened. Worm snot. Its power source must be drained. He got out of bed again. This time he had to rummage in his chest to find his game-vid.

He pulled out the dead power boosters from the cube, and replaced them with the ones from his game. Instantly, a skin-monster's face flashed on three sides of the cube.

It bared its teeth and winked, and then vid-zoomed in on its fangs. When it spoke, it was Taahmic's voice. "Beware my bite, if you are an unauthorized viewer. I will chomp off your head and eat your toes for breakfast."

Arrth laughed.

"If it's you, Arrth, check me out. I'm a skin monster. " The vid zoomed back out to show Taahmic's face. "I went to bed normal and woke up looking like this. Just about tweaked me. I know what you're thinking; I'm pretty ugly. Don't worry, your turn's coming. It's called the transition."

Thanks for the info, Arrth thought. It's about two days late.

"I'd tell you in person, but you're on vacation. My grandmother Meadowlark said that all Bigfoots lose their fur when they're young like us. It's the biological half of turning into an adult. The other half, the spiritual half, is the *Night Out.*"

Taahmic's voice roared and the cube went black.

What was wrong? Arrth shook the cube and held it to his ear.

A faint whooshing sound started and stopped. It started and stopped again, but louder. The third time he heard Taahmic's quick intake of air, before his breath whooshed out like a burst of wind on a stormy night.

Arrth sighed. The vid-cube worked fine. It was just his friend's special effects.

"I get to spend a night out." Taahmic's voice sounded low and mysterious. "In the daaaaaark. All alooooone." It was his best, If You're Not Good, The Skin Man Will Get You, voice.

Arrth grinned.

"Ooooooutside." Pause. "Beyoooooond the cloaking booooundaries."

Taahmic's skin-face reappeared on the cube. In his normal voice he said, "It all sounds pretty wormy."

"A night outside," Arrth whispered and almost missed what came next.

"By the time you get back, I should look like my normal self. Which means you'll miss seeing this beautiful face. That's reason one I made this vid. Now listen close. Reason two is top, top secret. Tomorrow is my official Night Out. Once I'm outside, I plan to visit the skin-town.

"It's my only real chance to get a look at the monsters up close. I know we were going to do it together, but you're gone, and this is my chance. Don't be mad." He smiled and wiggled his eyebrows. "If something happens, and I don't make it back, I wanted to say good-bye." Taahmic raised his hand, all his fingers clenched into a tight ball except for the little one. It stood straight up. "May moss never grow in your brain."

"Or in your ears," Arrth whispered and raised his own little finger in a final salute.

The vid clicked off. Arrth felt a tightening in his throat. The mystery solved. Taahmic had gone outside and hadn't come back.

The skin-monsters had captured his best friend. Killed him. Maybe ate him, too. Everyone knew they were flesh eaters.

His stomach churned, and he tasted bile.

That's what would happen to everyone in the valley once the cloaking devices failed. He pictured hordes of skin-faces swarming the valley. Shooting and capturing everyone. His father. His mother. The whole clan.

And it would be all his fault.

His fault because he had shown himself to the skin-face.

His fault, because he'd thrown the device at the skin-face.

His fault because he'd run away.

Well, if it was his fault . . . then it was his responsibility to get it back. He threw off the covers and hopped out of bed.

11: Almost Daybreak

ARRTH hesitated outside Uulmer's techno lab. Although he hadn't slept and it was almost morning, energy consumed him; his thoughts raced like an ant on hot coals.

Maybe it hadn't been such a good idea to come.

What if the techno wouldn't help him? Or couldn't? Still, what other choice did he have? Deep down in his hair follicles, he knew that his plan was the clan's only hope.

Crossing his toes, he pushed the entry request button, and waited. Nothing. He pushed the button again and started to bounce on the balls of his feet. His hands rhythmically slapped his thighs.

"Come on, Uulmer. Answer your door."

He held his breath until the door cloaker finally shimmered into a pale blue fog and dissipated. A distracted Uulmer appeared on the threshold.

Arrth pushed into the cave. "Quick. Close the door."

"I'm not closing the door until you get out. Go home. I'm busy."

"I just need a minute." To Arrth's embarrassment, his voice cracked.

"I don't have a minute."

"Please."

"What don't you understand? If I don't fix the perimeter cloaking device," Uulmer pointed to the chronometer carved into the wall, "in exactly five days, ten hours and sixteen minutes, the device will fail."

Arrth felt his eyes morph gray. "I think I can help."

"I don't have time for this." Uulmer rubbed his head, spiking his hair like a porcupine's.

"But it's my fault. I threw the device at the creature. That's how he got it."

"You did what?" Uulmer grabbed his head. "You idiot."

"I thought it was a rock."

Uulmer growled.

"It was an accident, but I have a plan."

"A plan?" Uulmer snorted. "You're only seventy-seven. You might have lost your fur, but you're still a cub. Don't be thinking you're an almost-adult. Your push through the barrier caused your premature transition, but it didn't give you brains. Now go away. This threat is real."

"I know it's real. Just listen." Arrth talked so fast his words tripped up against one another. "I'm the only one who's seen the creature up close. I can recognize it."

Uulmer's shook his head. "No. No. No. It's too risky."

"No, it's not. I'll find the monster. With or without your help. And I'll bring back the device."

"No. You're not going anywhere. Your parents would be furious."

"We won't tell them."

"We won't need to, because you're not going."

Arrth stomped his foot. "It's a good idea, and you know it."

"Good idea, wrong person to pull it off. Describe the creature. I'll send someone else. Someone older. That way the plan might have a chance of success."

"A: no one else can pass for a skin-face. B: who knows what it smells like? I'm the only one who can do this."

Uulmer's eyes clouded, and Arrth could see that he'd scored two important points. The older's lips pinched together and began to push in and out, almost at war with one another.

"It's my plan. It has to be me."

"I don't know," Uulmer said, rolling his head in circles.

"Come on. I'll be back before anyone knows I'm gone."

"You don't know what's out there. What those creatures are like."

"Then tell me."

Uulmer did. And he was right. The creatures sounded worse than horrible. They trapped, killed, and ate other creatures. They even killed one another.

"I don't care," Arrth said, sounding more confident than he felt. "I'm going."

Uulmer frowned. "You're sure no one knows you're here?"

"They think I'm in bed."

"This seems wrong, but. . ." Ulmer looked at the ticking chronometer. His eyes morphed from gray, to blue, back to gray and settled a light tawny brown. He shook his head and mumbled to himself. Finally he seemed to make up his mind. "It's a crazy plan, but you'll need to be prepared. Follow me."

The cave was a lot bigger than it appeared from the outside. Arrth followed Uulmer until it widened into a space full of fantastical experiments. Arrth paused in front of a huge holo-vid of the valley. It looked real, only miniature. He reached out and stuck his finger into the side of Mootak Mountain. It shimmered. A flicker of green light zapped him. He jumped back and almost knocked over a glass beaker of a blue solution that smelled like fermenting prairie grass.

"Hurry up." Uulmer's voice came from behind an obsidian partition. "For a younger, you sure are slow."

Arrth hurried to catch up.

"First thing you'll need is a cloth hide," Uulmer said.

The techno stopped in front of a life-size mosaic of a beautiful white-fanged female. "Isn't she magnificent," he said. He leaned forward and kissed the lips of the picture.

Eeeeeew, gross, thought Arrth. Uulmer spent too much time alone.

Overhead, a red light flashed. At the same time, the picture slid sideways into the stone wall. Where the picture had been seconds earlier now was an open doorway.

"Welcome to my weapons room."

12: Still Almost Daybreak

Five days, ten hours until device failure . . .

THE weapons room was a disappointment; just a giant walk-in closet lined with box-covered shelves and rows and rows of drawers.

Uulmer pulled a stiff blue cloth hide from a top shelf and handed it to Arrth. "Put it on. Skin-faces call them overalls. Your legs go there. This part hooks over your shoulders."

Arrth put on the overalls. The material felt funny rubbing against his skin, but they covered him better than the blanket and freed up his hands. More important, he didn't have to worry about it falling off every few steps.

"You'll need some techno tools," Uulmer said and pulled open a narrow drawer.

"Techno tools?" Arrth said.

Uulmer pulled two silver metal bands from the drawer. Arrth eyed them suspiciously. They looked a lot like the cub restraints his mom had made him wear until he was twenty. She said she didn't want him jumping from the tops of redwood trees. Taahmic had said she was overprotective. Arrth had agreed.

"Never take these off," Uulmer said.

"What are they?"

"Foot cloakers." Uulmer bent and snapped one band around Arrth's left ankle.

His foot instantly downsized to a thirteen-inch foot encased in a funny-looking, black, square-toed footboot.

He grinned. "Wow! What happened to my foot?"

"Your foot's still there. The footboot is an illusion."

Uulmer handed Arrth the second band. "See this tiny green button?"

"Yeah."

"You can morph the appearance of your foot to any size or shape. Just hold the cloaker over any skin-face footboot. Push the button down until you hear a click. Snip-snap, you've changed your foot style. Try it."

He set a small red sparkly footboot on the floor. It was odd and uncomfortable looking with a sharp point at the toe end and a spike under the heel.

"Skin-faces really wear these?" Arrth said.

Uulmer barked out a short laugh. "Its technical name is a high heel. The females wear them."

"I think I'll stick with the boots." Arrth slipped on the second band.

"Good call. Now go walk over there where the floor's dusty and check out your footprints."

"Double wormy," Arrth said. "My footprints are boot prints." He jump-kicked like a Yeti Ice Fighter and let out a surprised yelp when his invisible big toe clipped the wall. "Owwww, that hurt!"

Uulmer bark-laughed again. "Watch yourself, you still have big feet."

Next, the techno picked up a long box. Inside, several small thin yellow sticks lay in a neat row. He selected one and fiddled with it for a minute before handing it over.

Arrth took it and rolled it between his fingers. It was six-sided. One end had a tiny metal band stuffed with a round bit of pink rubber. The other end had a sharp point of wood with a black center. It looked pretty useless for a techno tool.

"What is this?"

"A locating device disguised to look like a common skin-faced tool they call a pencil." Then Uulmer held up a hand-sized rock. "I put an identifier like the one on the real thing. Close your eyes while I hide it."

Uulmer could have hid it a thousand times for the time he took scurrying from one part of the cave complex to another.

"What's taking so long?" Arrth said.

"Ready. Open your eyes. Twist the pink end and put the other end in your mouth."

Arrth stuck the pencil in his mouth and frowned. It tasted funny; a cross between wood and something metallic.

"Don't bite down on it."

"I'm not. What now?"

"The closer you get to the hidden device, the warmer the locater will get."

"Okay." Arrth turned towards the right. The point began to warm his tongue. He started forward and it grew warmer and warmer with every step until it felt like it was hot enough to burn his tongue. He leaned behind a potted plant, reached down, and picked up the test-rock.

"I found it."

"Good job. Here, give me the pencil." Uulmer twisted the end and stuck it into a flap sewn on the chest of Arrth's overalls. "Whatever you do, don't lose this. Pencils are a common skin-face tool. You don't want it to get mixed up with one of theirs."

"I won't. It must be almost daybreak. I better get going."

"Wait." Uulmer unlocked a drawer and held up a ring. "One last tool. This is a psychic ring. It will allow you to mental link with a skin-face."

"Does that mean I'll be able to read their minds?"

"No. Just to plant thoughts. But it's only for emergencies." Uulmer slipped on the ring. "You push the red stone and then press it against their skin, like this."

Uulmer grabbed Arrth's arm.

Suddenly Arrth felt an overwhelming desire to clap his hands.

Uulmer released his grip, and Arrth started enthusiastically clapping.

"You can stop now."

Arrth ignored him.

Ulmer grabbed his arm again and said, "Stop clapping."

Instantly, Arrth lost the desire and stopped. Snarfing weird.

"Planted thoughts are temporary. They fade in a few hours,"

Uulmer said.

They both looked at the chronometer.

Uulmer said, “Get out of here before I change my mind.”

“Thanks,” Arrth said and started for the exit.

“I’ll tell your parents I’ve drafted your services for an experiment to locate the cloaking device and that you can’t leave this cave until it’s over. You have three days.”

“Three days? I thought you said five.”

“I did, but I can only cover your nonappearance for so long. Then I’ll have to tell them.” His eyes morphed blue. “If you haven’t found the device by then, the clan will need time to evacuate.”

13: Mid Morning

Five days, nine hours until device failure . . .

ARRTH gazed down the steep, bare hillside. Nothing grew on it. No bushes. No trees. Not even a patch of grass. Foot-sliding straight to the bottom would be the fastest way down. Did he dare try it? The loose rocky shale would make for a snarking ride, but he'd never done it from this high up before. And nothing this vertical.

He calculated the drop. It was at least a hundred feet to the bottom where a wide flat black track hugged the edge of the hill. Was it a road? Uulmer had said to avoid them. Why?

It looked harmless. Plus it was a direct path to the skin-town. That meant no more getting lost and wasting precious time. Even though he stood there alone, his face grew warm with embarrassment. How had he managed to start off in the wrong direction that morning? He'd been halfway to the ocean before he realized his mistake and turned back.

Foot-sliding from this high up could be a another mistake. But to go up, around, and back down would take forever.

"Just go for it," he told himself. "You can do it."

He flexed his fingers, bent his knees, and edged his toes out over the edge. Taking one last gulp of air, he leaned forward. Whoosh! He was off. His arms flew up and flailed like he was flying. Sharp pebbles rained from his feet.

"Whooooaaaaaaa," he shouted. "Slow down. Slow down. Turn."

He shifted all his weight to his right foot. His descent slowed when he traversed right. A quick hop and a shift to his left foot. He turned left.

"Waaaahooo!" He was in control. This was the snarkiest!

Hop. Turn.

Hop. Turn.

Hop. Turn.

He was almost down. Just another twenty feet to go when he saw the boulder, straight ahead, protruding from the hillside. Where had it come from? It hadn't been there a minute ago. Had it? It didn't matter. Should he go left or right? He chose left.

Wrong choice. He hit the rock dead center and flew off in an arc. He came down on his knees and tumbled head over toes to the bottom.

He landed on the hard flat trail. The road. It was huge. Black and smooth. And it disappeared around turns in both directions. He hopped up, forgetting his fall. How could this road be dangerous? It just lay there on the ground with its white and yellow lines.

He jumped up and down on it. Nothing happened. It didn't react at all. Maybe it was the line markings that were dangerous.

He raised his right foot and put it down on the solid white line near the edge. The white stripe felt slick, cooler than the black, but definitely not dangerous. Then he noticed that his foot-cloaker hadn't left a bootprint. Oh no. Did they still work, or had he ruined them during his foot-slide? He went into the soft dirt and took two steps. Good. The cloakers still worked, just not on the hard road. He'd have to remember that.

So why had Uulmer said to avoid roads? Maybe the yellow lines were the problem. One way to find out. He moved to the center of the road, knelt down, and felt the line with his fingers. Then he slapped both palms flat onto the broken line and smiled. The lines were just color tints painted on the road.

"Oooo, what a scary road you are," he said, laughing.

The road began to vibrate.

What? He tried to stand, but tripped over his feet and fell flat on his face. Hard.

The road roared.

Arrth scrambled to his knees in time to see a huge metal monster bearing down on him. It blasted a battle cry and screeched. Smoke came from its feet. It smelled awful. Unnatural.

It slipped and slid sideways towards him.

He rolled like a log in a waterfall off the road and down a steep embankment. The rocky ground bit into his bare skin as he did a gravity tumble.

"Owwww!" He slammed into a boulder at the bottom. It knocked the breath out of him. He couldn't move.

Overhead the roaring stopped. Something squeaked. It was followed by a bang.

"What have I done?" a gruff voice said. "This is terrible. Are you there? Oh, please be okay."

To Arrth's horror, a skin-face male peered down from the top of the embankment.

"You okay, kid? Can you move?"

Arrth couldn't speak. He got to his feet and nodded. He had to make like a weasel and get out of there.

"Are you hurt?" The skin-faced man sounded worried. "Break anything?"

Arrth shook his head. This time he managed to squeak out a, "No." He frantically looked for an escape route. Nothing but the creek below.

"You sure?" The man sounded less worried now.

"I'm okay."

"Then tell me, what the heck you were doing out in the middle of the road on a blind turn."

"Feeling the yellow line?"

"What? Are you stupid or something? Do you realize I could've killed you? "

"Sorry."

"You could've killed me. I almost rolled my truck." Now the man sounded angry. Real angry. Just like his father did when he got mad at Arrth for doing something he considered foolish. "If I wrecked my truck, then what would I do for a living?"

"I said I was sorry." Arrth felt his eyes beginning to morph. At least the man stood too far away to see them darken, but he'd have to be careful when he reached the skin-village. It'd be stupid to get caught because he couldn't control his thoughts.

"Sorry. Sorry. That's all you kids have to say. If you were my boy, I'd beat a little respect into you." The man spit. "You climb back up here. I'm going to take you to your parents. They're going to pay for the dent in my door."

"I couldn't have dented your door. I didn't touch it."

"Don't get smart with me, boy. You'll sing a different tune when the police come for you. Now get your sorry backside up here."

Arrth didn't waste any time. He spun and raced toward the creek. He couldn't let the man catch him. If he did, they'd never let him go. He'd never find the device. The cloaking perimeter would fail and it would be the end of the clan's home. Forever.

"You come back here, you little brat."

Arrth splashed into the creek and didn't look back.

14: Noon

Five days, seven hours until device failure . . .

ARRTH forged a path parallel to the black road. His stomach grumbled and he wished he'd thought to bring food. It was hard to concentrate with his stomach and mind battling for attention.

Maybe if he drank enough water, it'd fill him up for a while. He climbed back down to the creek. Water skeeters skated to the far side of a shallow pool as he slurped up a bucket measure of water from the stream. It helped a little; not enough. Still hungry, he grabbed a couple handfuls of yellowed grass. Dry and tasteless roughage, but better than nothing. At least now he could concentrate on his mission.

First he had to infiltrate the creatures' lair called Willow Creek. How? Planning was difficult when he didn't know what to expect. The vid-books, Taahmic's stories, and the snatches of adult conversations he'd overheard all seemed a little off. Even Uulmer's advice seemed vague and sketchy.

Take the skin-faced man on the road. He hadn't acted like a monster when he thought he'd hit a kid with his rolling metal box machine. He'd sounded worried. Scared, even. He didn't get mad until he realized Arrth was okay.

Passing for a skin-face would be a lot more complicated than he'd thought. If he was going to have any chance of success, he needed to sift the facts from the myths.

He'd start with what he knew to be absolutely true about the creatures.

One. Skin-faces spoke the same language that he did.

Two. He looked enough like one for the skin-faced man to call him a boy. A boy must mean a younger.

Three. They didn't smell like rotten fish.

Four. The road wasn't dangerous, but what moved on the road could kill you.

Five. Skin-faces rode in noisy metal boxes that barreled down the roads.

Six. When skin-faces got mad, they sounded a lot like clan adults.

He frowned and kicked a rock over the bank. It seemed like he should already be there. Had he gone the right way? He was just about to turn around when he saw a green sign planted next to the road. One more thing to add to his list.

Seven. They used the same written language. So they couldn't be too stupid. The white printed letters on the primitive green sheet of metal read:

City Limits
Willow Creek
Population 1743
Elevation 590

Wow! One thousand seven hundred and forty-three skin-faces! All in one place!

His stomach twisted into a knot. What if he didn't pull it off? What if he failed? The clan was doomed.

"Stop thinking that way," he told himself. Time to start acting like an almost-adult. Time to find the cloaking device.

He put the pencil locater in this mouth and twisted it on. Nothing, just the unpleasant taste of metal and wood. Not close enough, yet. That's okay. He'd just keep it in his mouth and keep walking until he felt something. He rounded the bend and his mouth dropped open. The locator fell. He caught it before it hit the ground. Another sign sprouted by the road.

ADOPT A HIGHWAY
BIGFOOT LION'S CLUB

Lions! No, there couldn't be. Lions lived in packs. Fierce hunters.

Meat eaters. And they roamed this section of the road? Why would skin-faces adopt lions from across the ocean and bring them here? Did they plan to use them to hunt his clan?

Arrth swallowed. Things were more serious than he'd thought.

He tensed, ready to run for his life. His eyes darted everywhere at once. He had to get moving. He ran. Around the next turn he stopped again. He forgot the lions. Forgot his mission.

Strange square dwellings sprouted in rows along the paved road. Big ones. Small ones. Tall ones. All painted different colors. And roads. Lots of roads, criss-crossing each other, filled with the metal-boxes-on-wheels. All in constant motion.

He stared, rooted to the scene, unable to move.

This was totally snarfing amazing.

None of the skin-faces in their boxes ran into each other. Were they mind-linked? That didn't make sense. They were supposed to be primitive, like the green sign at the edge of the village.

And then there were the creatures on foot. Dozens of them. They stood in clumps on corners. Walked on the narrow gray paths that stretched along the road. He dry swallowed. His knees went weak at the thought of having to walk past them. Worse, he might have to talk to them.

He felt eyes on him. Better get moving, he told himself. Try to blend in. Find the device and get out before one of them discovers that he's not one of them. He shoved the pencil device back into his mouth and forced himself to move forward.

His skin prickled and he tried not to shudder. He scooted past two men and almost ran into a tiny, hunched female coming out a square door. Her hair was dark gray like Meadowlark's. She must be an old-old.

"Excuse me," Arrth said and hurried on, amazed at the variety of the creatures. They came in all shapes, but they all seemed to be adults like in his Skin-Face Slayer game.

It was mid-morning. Where were the youngers? He didn't see a single one. Then a horrible thought struck and he felt his heart throb in his toes. Maybe the stories were true.

Maybe they did eat their young.

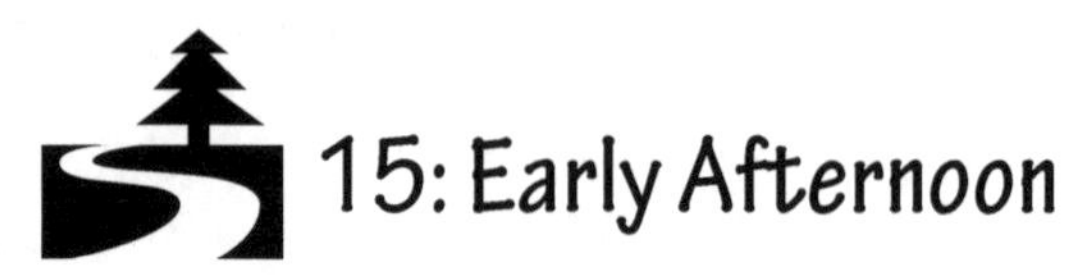

15: Early Afternoon

Five days, six hours until device failure . . .

ARRTH grinned. None of the creatures to seemed to notice him. Like he was invisible or that he belonged. He lengthened his strides. Infiltrating the skin-epicenter had been easier than he'd imagined.

The farther he walked, the larger Willow Creek got. It mushroomed along both sides of the road like uncontrollable mold spores.

More box dwellings: tall, squat, small, and big.

More roads: black paved, graveled gray, and hard packed dirt.

More rolling boxes: long and short and every color of the rainbow.

Willow Creek was huge. Of course, it had to be if one thousand, seven hundred and forty-three skin-faces lived there. Ulmer's estimate of a hundred creatures had been way off. Ten times off. And ten times off the time it would take to locate the skin-thief.

That was okay. He had the locator and plenty of time. He hoped.

His nose tingled. A familiar sweet fragrance floated on the breeze. Apples. His stomach rumbled and he picked up his pace. Several boxes of fruit and vegetables sat on the path in front of tall box dwelling. It had a sign: Grocery Store. "Grocery" was a new word, but he knew what it meant. Food. Apples, pears, grapes, tomatoes, and cucumbers begging to be eaten.

One particular shiny red apple looked absolutely perfect. And huge. He reached for it, but caught his furless monster reflection in the hard clear window and froze. Oooooh, talk about worm slime ugly!

He snatched a pear instead. His teeth sunk into its soft sweet flesh. Juice spurted and ran down his chin. So good.

A pungent musky odor floated into his nostrils. It reeked so strong he could almost taste it.

"You're supposed to pay before you eat," a high-pitched nasal voice said. "But I'm guessing you're not from around here."

Arrth turned to face the voice, the source of the overpowering stench, and went slack-jawed.

In front of him stood a very strange-looking skin-faced male. Not much taller than Arrth, but big around like a pregnant she-bear with quadruplets. So big in the belly, he looked like he'd swallowed ten watermelons. The top of his head was hairless, but a bushy black swatch of black hair grew over his lips.

"You look hungry. Let me buy you another pear." The creature smiled, revealing big flat teeth.

The monster sounded kind, but if Arrth still had fur, it would be bristling.

The skin-face reached into his clothes and produced a handful of metal disks. He dropped one into the slot of a small wooded box labeled, paybox. "That should cover your snack. I hate to see a boy hungry. Go ahead. Have another."

Arrth selected a second pear. He shoved the whole thing in his mouth, chewed twice, and swallowed.

"You are hungry. How about an apple?"

"No thanks."

"Grapes?"

"Okay."

The skin-man dropped more metal disks into the box and picked a huge clump of sweet green grapes.

Arrth began eating, a handful at a time.

"What's your name? Shouldn't you be in school?"

School? What was school?

"Speak up, boy. No one's going to hurt you. In fact, I'm here to help you." Then the skin-face did something so strange Arrth almost bolted. The man opened his mouth wide, pushed his teeth half out between his lips, clattered them, and then used his tongue to pull them back into his mouth. "What's a matter? Cat got your tongue?"

Gross, thought Arrth.

"Your name?"

"Arrth."

"Okay, Arthur. I know this isn't a holiday. So why aren't you in school?"

"The name's Arrth. I don't go to school."

"Home-schooled, huh? Where are your parents?"

"I . . ." His voice faltered. What was the skin-face talking about now? "I don't go to home school."

A big smile lit the fat man's face. "Not in school, you say. Are your parents inside, shopping?" he asked, pointing into the store.

"I don't have parents," Arrth lied, hoping the man would lose interest and just leave.

"Hmmmmmm. No school. No parents. Excellent, Arthur. This is your lucky day. I can help you." He reached into his pocket, drew out a small rectangular pink thing. He flipped it open and began to talk at it. "Meeker here."

Now that was wormy, thought Arrth. A mini-talker.

"Yes, I have a young man here who needs a temporary home. I know you wanted a toddler, but do you think you can handle a preteen?"

Pause.

"Good. I'll transport him myself." He closed the mini-talker. To Arrth he said, "This is your lucky day. Until things get sorted out, Maria and Mick Woods are your new foster parents."

"I don't need parents."

"And tomorrow we'll get you enrolled at the Trinity Valley Elementary School."

"I don't need school."

"I hear you. No one likes school, but it's a necessary evil." Meeker rubbed his chin.

"I'd say you'll fit in the seventh grade just fine." He stepped closer, grabbed Arrth's arm and stepped on his invisible right foot.

Arrth yelped and tried to pull free, but the skin-face's grip pinched harder.

"Let me go!"

"What's going on here, Meeker?" a deep mellow voice asked. "This kid giving you trouble?"

16: Early afternoon

Five days, six hours until device failure . . .

AFTERNOON, Deputy Sheriff Brown," Meeker said, releasing his grip on Arrth's arm.

Arrth stepped back and turned toward the new voice. Another skin-faced male. This one didn't look so harmless. The path in front of the grocery suddenly felt a little too crowded.

How snarfing weird.

The two creatures looked like different species. Deputy Brown was thin and towered over the short, fat Meeker. The officer had a full head of wavy brown hair. Meeker's head was bald. Deputy Brown's tanned skin glowed. Meeker's pale skin resembled the flesh of an overripe apple with age spots. The only thing they had in common besides standing erect on two legs was their calm, dark brown eyes.

"Met your quota?" Meeker asked, smiling wide. "Or do you still have a few tickets to write before you're done for the day?"

Deputy Brown frowned.

Meeker winked. "Don't worry. We're both public servants. I'll keep it on the Q.T."

"Who's the boy?" Deputy Brown asked.

"Why you asking?"

"He fits the description of a 911 call from earlier today."

Arrth dry swallowed. He had just got to town and it seemed like he was already tied up in a nest of unfriendly rattlesnakes. He didn't have time for this. He had to find the cloaking device.

"What's he supposed to have done?" Meeker asked, giving Arrth a side-glance.

Deputy Brown cleared his throat. "He fits the description of a boy playing chicken on the road west of town. Almost caused a wreck."

Meeker slapped his meaty hand on Arrth's shoulder. "Not this boy. Arthur's been with me all morning. I just stopped to buy him a snack before I took him over to the Woods. He's going to be their new foster kid."

The warning pressure of the man's hand slid to Arrth's neck. Then came a hard pinch. A shiver raced down his back. Why was Meeker lying?

"You're a lucky boy." The deputy narrowed his eyes to study Arrth's face. "Not everyone gets a second chance in this world." He laced his fingers together and bent his wrists back. Crick. Crack. It sounded like twigs snapping. "That boy on the road used up his when he ran. "

"Wish I could be more help," Meeker said. He shrugged and looked at his wrist. "But we're already late. Got to go."

The officer cracked his knuckles again, still staring hard at Arrth.

"When I find that boy, he'll be sorry he ever stepped onto that pavement. That is, if he's still alive when I get to him."

What did the man mean, still alive? Arrth's mouth went dry. Was that Deputy Brown's job? To catch and kill people who walked on the road?

It didn't make sense. No, it couldn't be true. Or could it?

He'd have to go along with Meeker for the moment. He wouldn't contradict the fat man's lies, but once the officer left, he'd say good-bye and get on with his search.

"I've got to find that boy before he causes a serious accident." Officer Brown climbed back into his white rolling box decorated with green stripes and a shield that read, Humboldt County Sheriff. With a final nod, he zoomed off.

Meeker grabbed Arrth's arm. "So, you're a trouble-maker? Well, you'd better not cause me any trouble. Now come on."

Arrth pulled away. "I don't want to go with you. I have things to do."

Meeker rubbed his head like it hurt. "Just get in the car."

"Car? You mean this?" Arrth asked and pointed to the maroon metal-box-on-wheels.

"Don't play stupid. Now get in or I'll call the nice deputy back and tell him that in addition to your other mischief, I caught you shop-lifting."

"What are you talking about? I didn't pick up a shop."

Meeker sighed. "Enough of your nonsense! Make your choice. Come with me or it's juvie jail for you. I guarantee you'll be a lot happier at the Woods. They won't lock you up and toss away the key."

Some choice. Go with the creepy Meeker or get locked up.

Arrth frowned. It would be easier to outrun the fat man than the deputy. So for the moment he'd go along with Meeker. Then he'd escape . . . after his ride in the car contraption. What a snarfy story he'd have to tell when he got back.

Meeker opened a side-panel on the car. It shrieked in protest. He waited while Arrth got into the car.

A little hot pink bubble-car zipped beside Meeker's car. The driver, an almost-adult female with big hair, hopped out with a really big rat clutched under her arm. The rat spotted Meeker and started yapping like a dog. It wriggled free, raced to Meeker's feet, and bit him.

Meeker moved like lightning. He jumped in the car, slammed the door, and slid in behind the wheel, gasping for breath. His pale face, beaded with sweat, looked even whiter than before.

The female tapped on the window and shouted, "I'm sorry. I don't know what got into Prince. He's never done that before. But don't worry. He's had his rabies shot."

Meeker waved her away.

"What was that?" Arrth asked.

"A blasted Chihuahua."

"A what?"

"A scrawny mutt." He touched something near the wheel. "I hate dogs."

The car started to hum and vibrate. Arrth clutched the seat, braced his legs, and held his breath.

"It's click it or ticket. So buckle up."

"Buckle up?"

"Jeez Louise," Meeker said and reached across Arrth to pull a flat rope from under the seat. It had a metal tab and the man clicked it into a small metal holder.

Arrth didn't like being strapped to the seat. His hand felt for the buckle. He'd have to know how to release it. When it came time to escape, he'd need to move fast. His fingers felt something in the center of the buckle. He pushed it and heard a click.

"Keep your seatbelt buckled. You don't want to give Deputy Brown an excuse to stop us, do you?"

"I just wanted to see how it worked." He reclicked it.

Meeker backed the car into the street.

Until Arrth had the opportunity to escape, he may as well enjoy the ride. He stuck the pencil locater device in his mouth. Instantly the tip grew warm. Then warmer. He must be close. Frantically he scanned the street. There were at least ten square dwellings in range. It had to be in one of them, but which one?

The tip turned hot.

"Stop the car," he shouted.

Meeker ignored him. The car picked up speed and the pencil point turned cold.

"Worm snot!"

"What?"

"Nothing," Arrth muttered, angry that he'd let the first skin-face he met capture him.

17: Mid Afternoon

Five days, four hours until device failure . . .

ARRTH stared out the car window, memorizing landmarks that zoomed past. Once he escaped Meeker, he'd backtrack to the place where the pencil locator had given a positive reading. So far they'd driven by the Bigfoot Motel.

Turned north on the Bigfoot Highway.

Travelled down a hill.

Raced past The Bigfoot Den and Bigfoot Trailer Resort.

The road straightened and flattened. Several huge gravel mountains sprouted on the right. The Bigfoot Gravel Company.

"What's with all the Bigfoot names?" he asked.

Meeker gave him a sideways glance. "You aren't from around here, are you?"

Arrth shook his head.

"This is Bigfoot Country."

"Aren't they just make-believe?"

Meeker laughed. the flesh on his neck quivered. "That's what some folk think. Makes them feel safe. But I always say, where there's smoke, there's fire."

"What's a smoky fire have to do with Bigfoot?"

"It means, if there were no Bigfoots, there'd be no talk about them."

"So you think they're real?"

Meeker nodded. "As real as you and me. Mark my words, one day a Bigfoot will line my pockets with gold."

Arrth ground his teeth. He'd had enough of Meeker. Now that they were out of town, it was time to make his escape. Once he was free, he'd hide until dark, and then return for the perimeter device. It'd be easier to blend into the night shadows and make his move without so much adult interference. But first he had to get away from Meeker.

He rubbed his fingers and felt his ring. Why hadn't he thought of it earlier? Before he got into Meeker's car. All he had to do is activate the ring and command Meeker to let him go. The effects were supposed last for at least twelve hours. By then, he'd have the device and be home. Way before Meeker even knew what hit him.

So snarking simple!

He'd been stupid for not thinking of it sooner. Arrth pushed in the stone on the ring, reached over, and put his hand on Meeker's bare head.

PULL the car to the side of the road and stop, thought Arrth.

Meeker steered the car to the side of the road. He looked at Arrth. "Why are we parked on the side of the road?"

Jumping worm snot. It worked. Arrth un-clicked the seat belt and fumbled to open the car door.

"What are you doing?" Meeker reached across Arrth to pull the door closed.

The car lurched forward.

Arrth grabbed for Meeker's hand. At the same time he thought, *FORGET WHO YOU ARE. FORGET WHAT YOU'RE DOING.*

Meeker's hand flapped like he was swatting a swarm of mosquitoes.

Arrth missed. Instead of connecting with skin, he'd grabbed a handful of cloth.

He tried again. Meeker batted his hand away.

"Quit it! You'll like living with the Woods. They're nice people."

Arrth reached a third time for Meeker. Forget who you are. Forget what you're doing.

The car swerved. Without the seat belt, Arrth slid. His hand flailed to catch his balance. He missed Meeker's hand again. Somehow he smacked his own left wrist.

"Noooooo," he moaned.

Vainly, he tried to break the connection. To think another thought, but it was too late.

He turned to the stranger driving the car. “Excuse me, but who are you? Where are we going? I can’t seem to remember.”

18: Morning

Four days, twelve hours until device failure . . .

ARRTH drifted at the edge of sleep; almost awake, but not quite. Comfortable. Warm. The bed soft. The blanket fuzzy like a bear cub's fur . . . and a delicious fragrance floated in the air.

His eyes flew open. The last thing he remembered, a skin-monster had been shouting at him. Insisting that he'd like the Woods family.

Is that where he was?

His gaze darted around the strange pod. It was square, tinted yellow, and had a flat ceiling. A shelf on the far wall displayed an array of intricate wood carvings; owls, raccoons, chipmunks, and deer.

Then it all came back to him.

The road.

The skin-creature Meeker, threatening to lock him up.

His disastrous attempt to use the psychic ring.

He shivered and threw back the covers of the bed. Time to get out of there. Now. Find the device. Get back to the valley. Save the clan. He smiled. He'd be a hero.

Now where were his overalls? They'd disappeared.

Footsteps.

He leapt back into bed and pulled the covers up to his chin.

Knock. Knock.

"Are you awake, Arthur? It's time to get up," came a soft female voice. The primitive wooden door popped open and the skin-woman stepped into the room -- a tiny, curly-headed skin-woman. She looked fragile; not even close to dangerous. If he sat on her she'd probably snap in two.

Her arms were loaded with cloth, and a pair of white footboots dangled from one hand. She smiled, and he could tell she was nervous. Her eyes were bright blue like the sky on a summer day.

"Did you sleep well?" she asked. "You sure were tired. Too tired to even eat dinner last night."

Arrth couldn't remember anything. The last fourteen hours were a total blank.

"You even passed up dessert. I've never met a boy who didn't like my apple pie. Don't feel bad. I saved you a piece."

"Thanks, but I don't eat apples. I'm allergic."

She gave him a funny look. "That's too bad. We have an orchard and the trees are loaded this year." She set her armload of cloth on the foot of the bed. "I brought you some clean clothes. I hope you like red."

"Sure."

"Good. I got you a red shirt, new blue jeans, white socks, underwear, and a pair of tennis shoes. Your overalls were pretty grungy so I threw them away."

Arrth didn't know what to say, so he said nothing.

"Get dressed and come down to the kitchen for breakfast."

"Where's the kitchen?"

She laughed. "Right where it's always been, at the bottom of the stairs. Don't waste time. Mr. Meeker is picking you up in forty-five minutes for school. You don't want to be late on your first day."

"I don't want to go to school."

She smiled. "I know the first day at a new school can seem brutal, but don't worry. You'll make lots of new friends."

She closed the door.

Arrth flung back the covers and jumped out of bed for the second time. He eyed the mysterious pile of clothes. With the overalls gone, he'd have to figure out what went where.

"This shouldn't be too complicated," he muttered. He examined each piece. The blue jeans looked like the bottom half of the overalls. He slipped them on. Now the red one -- the shirt. It must go on the top half of him. It took three tries to get it right. Or what he hoped was right.

Next came the white socks. Plural. She must have meant the two long white cloth tubes. What were they for? He did a quick inventory. He had two eyes, two ears, two legs, two feet, two arms, and two hands. The tennis shoes were obviously for his feet and his arms and legs were already taken care of. He wasn't stupid enough to think they were for his eyes or ears, so . . . the socks must be for his hands. He'd put them on last, once he was fully dressed.

Following Uulmer's instructions, he changed the foot-cloakers to look like the tennis shoes and hid the real shoes under the bed.

The one last piece must be the underwear. It looked kind of like his mother's moss gathering bag, minus the handle. But it couldn't be. It wouldn't hold anything with the two big holes in the bottom. He squinted. There were words written on the top opening. "Fruit of the Loom."

Fruit?

No. The skin-woman had said they were clothes. That meant he was supposed to wear them. Well, there was only one patch of bare skin left to cover. He whistled, feeling downright snarky. He'd solved the mystery. The two holes must go over his two ears.

Finally dressed, he went down the stairs that led straight into the kitchen. The howls and growls from his stomach convinced him to delay his escape until after breakfast. That way he'd have plenty of energy to find the device and return home.

He'd eat fast and leave before Meeker arrived to take him to school. He grinned. It was a good plan.

He paused on the bottom step and peeked into the kitchen.

"Maybe we should let him stay home today and get used to us," Maria said. "He could start school on Monday. Please, Micky."

"No," a man's deep voice replied.

Arrth stepped into the room and his eyes widened.

The male was big for a skin-creature. Not slug big like Meeker, but strong big. He lifted a cup to his lips and the muscles in his arms flexed under his skin. His hands were large and calloused. Like Meeker, he was bald, but he had bushy eyebrows and was dark-skinned.

"Maria, remember what Meeker said. One of the conditions of foster parenting is to see that the foster child is in school."

Mick and Maria noticed Arrth at the same time.

She giggled.

Mick raised an eyebrow, frowned, and shook his head. "This was your idea, you deal with it. It's already late. I have to leave for work."

19: Morning

Four days, twelve hours until device failure . . .

MICK!" Maria said, sounding annoyed. "Say good-bye before you go."

"Bye," Mick said and left, slamming the door behind him. Dishes in the sink rattled.

"What did I do?" Arrth asked. "Why's he mad?"

"He's not mad at you. It just seems that lately, he's lost his sense of humor. That's all."

"Why? What's supposed to be so funny?"

"I'd say it's either the socks on your hands or the underwear on your head. Run upstairs and put them on right. Be quick about it or you won't have time to eat before Mr. Meeker arrives."

"Can't I eat first? I'm really hungry." His stomach gurgled in support.

"It won't take you but a second to change," she said.

"Change into what?"

She smiled, but didn't answer. Instead she pointed to the stairs.

Upstairs, Arrth still didn't have a clue what do with the socks. Or the underwear. So he stuffed them into the pair of tennis shoes under the bed. He was back downstairs in record time. Ready to eat. Ready to complete his mission.

That's when he remembered the pencil-shaped locater device. What had happened to it?

"I had a pencil. Did you see it?" he asked.

"Sit down and eat these pancakes before they get cold." She plopped down a plate on the table. It looked like a stack of giant fungus mushrooms. Not his favorite. At least these didn't smell like the ones his mother fixed. "I've already buttered them, but I'll let you put the syrup on."

"I need my pencil."

"Don't worry, we have lots of them. Now eat." She grabbed a glass crammed with pencils, and set it next to his plate. "Here, take one of these."

"You don't understand," he said. "I don't need just any pencil. I need my pencil. The one I brought with me last night."

"I don't remember your pencil, but if one was laying around I would have put it here. Mick would have done the same."

"Then which one is mine?"

"I don't know. You can figure it out while you eat. It's too bad you don't like apples. I make fresh sauce everyday. It's Mick's favorite. He can't get enough of it."

Arrth picked up a pancake with his fingers and crammed the whole thing in his mouth at once. It was so good, he moaned.

"Arthur, use your fork."

Fork? He swallowed. Was it the silver-pronged weapon next to his plate? He picked it up.

She smiled. "Don't you want syrup?"

"Sure," he said. "Can you put it on, while I sort through the pencils?" He grabbed one and tried to twist its end. Not it.

He tried a second one. Not it, either.

Or the third.

Or the fourth.

"Is this enough syrup?" she asked.

Arrth nodded and stabbed a pancake with the fork. It was a little awkward, but he managed to get the whole thing in his mouth. A sweetness that he'd never imagined exploded in his mouth.

"Don't take such big bites. You'll choke."

"No, I won't." He stabbed a third pancake. "They're really good."

He finished the last pancake and tested the last of the pencils at the same time.

"Are there any more?"

"Pancakes, yes." She slid two more onto his plate. "Pencils, no."

What was he going to do? There was no way he'd find the device without the locater. Willow Creek was too big. Plus there were way too many skin-faces. He swallowed another pancake.

Maybe he'd lost the pencil during his blackout? It could still be in Meeker's car.

A horn blasted outside.

Maria looked out. "It's Mr. Meeker." She handed Arrth a paper bag. "Here's your lunch. Have a good day."

Arrth bit his lip and nodded. He must have dropped the pencil in the car. Okay, he'd take the ride to school, but once he found his pencil, that was the last he'd see of Meeker. For good.

20: Morning

Four days, ten hours until system failure . . .

"WE'RE here," Meeker said and stopped the car between two white lines on an unbelievably huge paved section of the road. It was big like a meadow. Several cars of all shapes and sizes parked in neat straight rows.

"Great," Arrth said, thinking he couldn't wait to get a breath of fresh air. Meeker's stench was even stronger this morning. What had he bathed in? A rotting compost pile?

The inconvenience had been worth it. He'd spotted the locater on the seat when he got in the car. Luckily he hadn't sat on it. Now it was clutched tight enough to turn his knuckles white. One thing was for sure, he wouldn't let it out of his sight again.

"Your classroom's over there," Meeker said and pointed to a long reddish brown building. "It's the junior high."

THUD! A round orange orb bounced off the window and down the front of the car. Startled, Arrth flinched. Meeker leaped out like a she-bear protecting her cubs.

"Hey, watch that!" he shouted. "This car is a classic. You want to pay for a new paint job?"

A boy grabbed the orb. "What are you talking about? It's a junk heap." He took off, bouncing the ball while he ran.

Meeker whipped out his handkerchief and furiously rubbed the car where the orange thing had hit it. He muttered angrily, "What am I doing in this job? I hate kids."

Arrth slipped out of the car. Meeker didn't even look up.

What snarking luck. The truant man was too smertzed with his car to notice.

Taking one step at a time, Arrth inched backwards. When he'd put a good stone's throw distance between them, he turned. Instead of taking off like he'd planned, he stood rooted to the spot. Amazing.

Skin-kids. Lots of them. Everywhere. Most stood on the pavement behind the junior high school building. Huddled in groups.

Jumping over flying ropes.

Swinging from chains.

Laughing and having fun.

Together.

One boy bounced a ball and threw it at hoop on a pole. Arrth smiled. It kind of looked like the Slam Ball he and Taahmic used to play.

His throat tightened. It wasn't fair. These creatures had lots of kids their own age. He bet they didn't appreciate having someone to hang with. Or play with. Or talk to when things got rough. They didn't know what it was like to be the only one. He wished . . .

He shook himself. What was wrong with him? Jealous of a bunch of skin-monsters? Not even. He was too mature and focused on his hero's mission to even care about the fun skin-kids had.

Now that he had the pencil device, it was time to get on with the retrieval of the missing cloaking mechanism. Find it. Get it. Take it home.

A hand clamped on his neck. "There you are. I should have figured you were checking out the girls," Meeker said, and laughed.

Shivers ran down Arrth's neck. Why hadn't he just taken off?

Meeker pushed him. "Your classroom is this way."

Their path took them along the edge of the play area. That's when Arrth caught the faint scent of peppermint. He stopped. Meeker bumped into him. Worm snot! Now all he could smell was Meeker.

He scanned the yard. The skin-thief must be a kid. It made sense, now that he thought about it. It hadn't been tall like a skin-adult, but closer to his own height. Moving away from Meeker, he leaned into the breeze and sniffed.

Yes. There it was again. The sweet mint smell of the meadow on a hot summer day. He grinned, the skin-thief stood within his sight.

A tall man wearing short pants walked over. "Brought Miss H.

another new student, I see." The right corner of his mouth curled up and he winked three times.

Meeker's pasty skin turned red. "Just doing my job, coach."

"Sure you are," the man said, laughed, and punched Meeker in the arm. To Arrth, he said, "You're a tall one. Play basketball?"

"No."

"Doesn't matter. By the time the season starts I'll have you ready. We're in desperate need of a center." He waved to the boy with the ball. "Hey, Travis."

The boy bounced the ball as he ran toward them. "Yeah, coach. You wanted me?" He had dark brown wavy hair. His jaws chomped up and down while he talked.

"Nope, just the basketball."

Arrth caught a whiff of peppermint. Was this boy the skin-thief? Maybe. He tried to imagine him covered in the spotted cloth hide. It could be, but he wasn't sure.

"Toss the new kid the ball," the coach said.

Travis threw it. The ball slammed into Arrth's bare palms and he yelped. He dropped it and shook his hands to ease the tingling. The ball rolled away.

Travis laughed. He snatched it, bounced it twice and shot it back to Arrth. This time Arrth caught it.

"See if you can throw the ball through the hoop," the coach said.

"Yeah," Travis said with a sneer. "I'd like to see that."

Sure you would, Arrth thought. He didn't care if he made some team, but the laughing boy's face made him want to hit it. This Travis probably was the skin-thief. Well, he'd show him.

He studied the distance, considered the light breeze, and took aim at the metal ring. He tossed the ball high and watched. It soared in an arch, came down, hit the ring, and bounced off to the side.

"Nice shot, " Travis said.

"Not bad," the coach said. He reached in his pocket, took out a tiny plastic box, and flipped it open. He raised it to his lips and tapped. A little white pill dropped into his mouth. "Want a mint?"

Another strong mint scent tingled Arrth's nose.

"Later, " Meeker interrupted. "I need introduce Arthur to his teacher before class starts."

"Think about it," Coach said. "Work with me and come basketball season, you'll be our starting center."

Arrth looked past the man to Travis. The boy scowled. He noticed Arrth's stare and mouthed just low enough for Arrth to hear, "You're dead, chemo-boy."

Arrth swallowed. He shouldn't be surprised. Uulmer had warned him that skin-faces were vicious. For no reason at all, now Travis wanted to kill him.

Not watching where he walked, he bumped into another, sweeter pepper-minted person. He turned. It was a female skin-kid.

"Hi, I'm Tamara. What's your name?"

"Arrth."

"Art. I like that name. It sounds strong and at the same time, sweet." She moved closer and stepped on his invisible toes.

He tried not to yelp and wriggled them from under her shoe.

"Ooooh," she said and giggled. "For a second there the ground felt all soft and squishy. No one's ever made me feel that way before." She smiled and touched his arm. "Don't worry about Travis. He's just mad because he's been the team center for the last two years. He'll get over it."

21: Still Morning

Four days, nine hours and forty-five minutes until system failure . . .

GOOD morning class," Ms. Hammerhead the teacher said. She was tall, sharp-faced, and wore her hair pulled back in a tight knot like a redwood burl bulging from a tree trunk. "We have a new student, Arthur Ford."

Artth stood uncomfortably at the front of the classroom. The skin-kids were seated in four neat rows and they all stared at him like he was a marsh freak. He hoped spending a few hours at school would be worth it. That he'd follow the peppermint boy home after school and see if he had the device. If he hid, Arrth would retrieve the device and be on his way before nightfall.

"Let's welcome Arthur," Ms. Hammerhead said and raised her hands in front of her chest. She started to clap.

The girls in the class enthusiastically joined in. The boys glared.

"Arthur," she said. "It's tradition in my class to play a little game of twenty questions with a new student." She looked at the class. "Who wants to go first?"

Every one of the girls' hands shot up.

"Katie," Ms Hammerhead said and pointed to a petite blond girl in the second row. "And don't forget to introduce yourself before you ask your question."

"Hi, I'm Katie." The girl reminded Arrth of Maria. She was small and had worried gray eyes. But she didn't sound worried when she spoke. "Does your family call you Arthur, or do you have a nickname?"

"My family calls me Arrth."

"Hi, I'm Jenny. Have you been sick? Did you have chemo? Is that why you don't have hair?"

"No, I cut it because ..." Arrth tried to think of a good excuse for his baldness. "It was extra hot this summer."

"Hi, I'm Tamara. We've already met." She winked. This skin-girl reminded him of someone, but he couldn't place who. She had long wavy brown hair and soft brown eyes. "Do you have a girlfriend?"

The class laughed.

"Give it a rest," Katie said. "He just got here."

"Let's hear from a boy," Ms. Hammerhead said. "Travis."

"What? I didn't raise my hand."

Ms. Hammerhead's smile morphed into a tight line. "It's your turn to ask Arthur a question."

Travis humphed. His eyes narrowed and his lips curled into a sneer. "Hello. My name is Travis and I have a question for you. Are you another one of Meeker's bogus runaways?"

"Huh? I don't know what you mean," Arrth said.

"You're the third kid since school started three weeks ago with a car name. First was Johnny Cadillac, then Tom Chevy, and now you're Arthur Ford. So are you one? Will you still be here next week? Or here for basketball season?"

"Travis!" Ms. Hammerhead's voice sounded sharp. "Take your seat. It's time for class to start. Sit over there," she said to Arrth and pointed to an empty seat behind Katie. "Class, take out a piece of paper. It's time for your spelling test."

Arrth squeezed into the chair attached to the desk. It swiveled. Everyone lifted the tops of their desks and rummaged inside. He opened his lid, too. It made a great shield between him and the teacher while he figured out what to do.

Desk lids shut in a series of snaps around the room. Most students had their paper and pencils ready.

"Pssst."

He looked toward the sound. Across the aisle, Tamara still had her desk open, but instead of looking for paper, she gawked at him.

"I'm so glad you're sitting next to me," she whispered. "Want to do lunch?"

He swallowed. She looked like she was about to eat him. A hot shiver ran down his spine and his stomach felt queasy. He dropped his desk lid and stared straight ahead.

Ms. Hammerhead had put on a pair of glasses and held a piece of paper.

"Don't forget to put your name at the top or you'll receive a zero," she said. She stared directly at Arrth. "I know it's your first day, but take the test anyway. We'll see what kind of a speller you are."

"I don't have any paper," he said.

Ripppp. Ripppp. Ripppp.

"Here's a piece," Katie said, handing back a sheet over her shoulder from in front.

"I've got extra," Jenny said, sending a piece over his shoulder from behind.

"Take mine," Tamara said, holding out a sheet to him from the left.

Too late he grabbed for all three and missed all three. They drifted to the floor like falling leaves. Arrth reached for the closest one and Travis stepped on it.

"Whenever you're ready," Ms Hammerhead said and tapped her book with a red pencil.

Travis kicked the paper. "Loser," he mouthed. He made his hand into an "L" shape and bounced it off his forehead.

"Ignore him," Katie said. "He's just a conceited want-to-be."

"Want-to-be-what?" Arrth asked.

"Silence!" Ms. Hammerhead ordered. "Anyone talking from here on receives an 'F.'"

22: Noon

Four days, seven hours until device failure . . .

ARRTH chose a seat in the lunchroom where he could keep an eye on Travis, who sat at an adjacent long table. Five other boys joined him. No one seemed to notice Arrth sat alone. They were too busy eating, talking, and laughing.

He didn't mind. It gave him time to think, watch, and plan.

Clearly, Travis had to be the skin-thief. None of the other kids seemed mean enough to shoot a defenseless rabbit.

"Hey, Travis," one boy said. "You still believe in Santa Claus and the Easter Bunny, too?"

All the boys hooted, except Travis.

"Go ahead, laugh," Travis said. "But wait until I get the reward money."

"Yeah, like you saw a Bigfoot," a second boy said.

"You must have been dreaming," a third boy said.

Travis flicked a piece of bread at him. "I have proof. It's in my locker."

"What kind of proof?"

Arrth leaned forward. Had Travis discovered the secret concealed in the rock?

"Art!" Tamara squealed and plopped down next to him; so close she almost sat on him.

Worm snot! He missed what Travis said.

"I get dibs on the other side," Jenny said and squished in on his left. Now he felt like a fly trapped in a spider web cocoon.

Both girls giggled.

"I bet you're a good dancer," Tamara said and elbowed him

playfully.

"Give him a little room so he can eat his lunch," Katie said and sat down across the table. The two girls glared at her, but they moved apart so at least he could breathe.

"Thanks," he said.

"Anything for you," Tamara said.

"Ditto," Jenny said.

Katie rolled her eyes. "What did you bring for lunch?" she asked.

He shrugged, opened his paper bag, and sniffed. His nose twitched. Interesting. Nutty and a scent of honey. He dumped it out onto the table. Wow. Skin-faces must like the taste of paper and plastic. Everything was wrapped in one or the other.

The three girls opened their lunch sacks and began arranging food on the table.

He picked up the square sandwich in the clear plastic bag, bit into it, and chewed. Part of it tasted good, but the plastic stuck in his teeth.

Tamara and Jenny giggled. Katie smiled, opened a similar looking plastic bag, and removed her sandwich from its wrapper. "They're better without the bag," she said and took a bite.

His face burned. He pulled off the remaining plastic, took a bite, and swallowed. "You're right, it is better."

All three girls laughed this time. Arrth joined them.

Travis came over to their table. "Why are you sitting with that loser?"

"Ignore him," Tamara said. "My brother's just jealous because Coach said you could play center."

"Travis is your brother?" Arrth said, wondering why he hadn't noticed earlier. They had the same dark brown curly hair, dark eyes, and olive skin.

"They're fraternal twins," Jenny said.

"Why don't you go back where you came from," Travis said and sneered.

"Just leave, Travis. You're such a pain," Tamara said. She linked her arm through Arrth's. "This is a private table."

Travis clenched his fist, but went back to sit with his friends.

Tamara grinned and scooted closer, giving Arrth's arm a squeeze.

He felt his skin blaze and tried to inch away from her.

Katie winked at him. "Did you hear about the new cheerleader tryout rules?"

"What do you mean?" Tamara asked. "New rules."

"Yeah, something about an official tryout uniform. I don't know," Katie said. "I only halfway overheard Ms. Sackey talking about it."

"That's not fair. I already bought my tryout outfit." Tamara let go of his arm and shoved what was left of her lunch back into its bag. "Are you sure?"

Katie shrugged. "Not really. I guess you could go ask her."

Tamara jumped up. "Come on, Jenny. We're going to talk to Ms. Sackey. She can't do this. It'll ruin everything."

The two girls left, and Katie started laughing.

"What's funny?" Arrth asked.

"Ms. Sackey is giving up being cheerleader advisor this year."

"Then why did you tell Tamara that Ms. Sackey had changed the rules?"

"I thought you might be ready for a Tamara break."

Arrth grinned. "Thanks, but won't she be mad when she finds out?"

"She doesn't like me anyway." Katie got up. "See you later. I have to go to the office to get a bus pass. You want my apple? I'm full."

"I'll have it," Travis said, having reappeared. He reached over and grabbed it. He took one bite and threw it at Arrth's head.

Arrth ducked.

The apple flew past his ear and hit another boy behind him.

"What the," the boy shouted and jumped to his feet. "Who threw that?"

Travis pointed at Arrth.

Arrth shook his head and pointed back to Travis.

The boy snatched the apple from the floor and threw it at Arrth. He ducked again. This time it hit Travis.

Someone yelled, "Food fight."

Suddenly the room was full of flying food and wadded-up lunch bags.

Half-eaten sandwiches.

Orange peels and squished bananas.

Fruit salad and chocolate pudding.

The boys from Travis's table all took aim at their friend. SPLAT! SPLOTCH! THUNK! SWISH! SQUISH! FIIFFT! Travis's shirt and pants transformed into big splotches of lunch.

Arrth furrowed his brow and concentrated. Yes. He was positive now. Travis was the skin-thief. He looked exactly like the skin-monster in the spotted cloth hide.

That had shot the long gun at the rabbit.

That had bit him.

That had stolen the cloaking device.

A loud whistle blasted inside the lunchroom.

"Stop this instant!" an adult voice yelled.

Silence. Everyone turned to stare at the tall man in the dark suit.

"Who started this?" the man said.

No one spoke.

"I'm waiting."

"The new boy," Travis said.

"Who said that?"

Travis raised his hand. "I did. I saw it all. That boy," he pointed at Arrth, "started it. He threw an apple at me."

"I see. But judging from the amount of muck on you, I'd say you were a major player, yourself." The man paused, surveyed the room and the remaining kids. Then he started pointing. "You. And you. You. And you." The last "you" was Arrth. "You can help Travis clean up this mess! The rest of you, get to class."

There was a mad dash for the exit.

"This is all your fault," Travis said. "You'll pay for it."

23: Mid Afternoon

Four days, five hours until device failure...

TIME for S.S.R. Take out your library books," Ms. Hammerhead said to the class. "Remember, this is your silent sustained reading time. No talking."

Arrth leaned forward and asked Katie, "What color is the book?"

"Any color," she said, but didn't turn around. "We're all reading different books."

"You can have one of mine," Travis said and tossed a thin shiny book onto Arrth's desk.

Arrth started to say he didn't want it, but the picture on the front cover stopped him. Four giant turtles brandished weapons and wore different colored headbands -- Teenage Mutant Ninja Turtles. Even though it was a thin book, it looked interesting.

He flipped open the cover. Wow. Colored pictures on every page. Wormy.

The classroom grew silent except for Ms. Hammerhead's clicking footfalls up and down the rows. When she got to Arrth she stopped. He looked up and she snatched his book.

"Comic books aren't books," she said and handed him a smaller thicker book: Johnny Tremain. "This is a real book."

Travis snickered.

Arrth expected another lecture, but the classroom door opened, letting in a familiar pungent musky stench. Meeker.

"Can I have a word with you, Ms. Hammerhead?" Meeker asked and motioned for her join him outside.

"Class, continue reading while I speak to Mr. Meeker. No talking."

"You look very lovely today," Meeker said. "Such loveliness is wasted on junior high . . ."

The door snapped shut.

"You look so lovely today, Ms. Hammerhead," Travis said in a high voice. "Would you like to examine my toenails? They're ever so lovely, too."

Everyone laughed. Even the girls.

Travis stood and held up a plastic bag with something brown inside.

"Here it is," he announced to the class. "Proof that Bigfoot exists." He pulled out the brown wad and held it up for everyone to see.

Arrth squinted. What was it? No, it couldn't be. Not fur. Not his fur.

"That looks like cow hair," one boy said.

"Or dog hair," another boy said.

Travis raised his voice. "I'm telling you, it's Bigfoot fur. I pulled it off a Bigfoot's back myself." He put the fur back into the bag.

"Sure you did," the first boy said. "And I bet it was hanging with a vampire, a werewolf, and the Loch Ness monster. Oh, and they were all drinking Coke and eating nachos." He grabbed the bag and tossed it to another boy.

Travis tried to grab it back.

Someone threw it at Arrth. Instinctively he caught it.

"Give it to me, you freak," Travis shouted. He lunged at Arrth.

Arrth jerked to the side and his desk teetered on two legs. He threw the bag. At the same time he leaned forward to regain his balance. He might have been successful if Travis hadn't given him a push.

CRASH! Down he went, desk and all.

"What's going on?" Ms. Hammerhead demanded, stepping into the room. Meeker was right behind her.

Arrth scrambled to his feet and righted his desk in time to see her snatch the fur bag mid-air and hand it to Meeker.

"Hey that's mine," Travis said. "It's my Bigfoot hair."

"Will someone tell me what's going on here?" Ms. Hammerhead said.

Her fierce glare could scare termites out of a rotten log, thought

Arrth.

"They were talking about Bigfoot," Jenny said in a quiet voice. "And the Loch Ness monster. Werewolves and vampires."

Meeker eyes narrowed into slits. He slid the bag into his pocket, and left.

Ms. Hammerhead's lips curled into a smile, but her eyes still glared.

"So, this class is interested in monsters." Her smile grew huge. "I have the perfect solution. Each of you will write a four-page paper on your favorite monster. It's due Monday morning. No excuses."

The class groaned.

She looked at Arrth. "As a newcomer, your report topic is Bigfoot."

She went to her desk and picked up a stack of white envelopes. She handed one to Travis, one to Arrth, and one each to three other boys. "Principal Morris asked me to remind those of you involved in the fiasco at lunch to have these letters signed by your parent or guardian and returned on Monday. Detention will be Tuesday and Wednesday of next week."

24: 4 PM Late Afternoon

Four days, three hours until device failure . . .

THERE were only two empty seats on the big yellow bus when Arrth got on. One at the back, next to Travis. The other in the middle, next to Katie.

"Take a seat," the female bus driver said. "I have a schedule to keep and the school don't pay overtime."

Arrth headed for the seat next to Katie. "Can I sit here?"

"Sure." She moved closer to the window.

It seemed like every few minutes the bus stopped. Each time its door wheezed open, more kids got off. He hoped Travis and Tamara would get off soon so he could follow them home and retrieve the cloaking device.

"I hate weekend homework," Katie said, interrupting his thoughts.

"What do you mean?"

"The monster report due Monday morning."

"Oh, those. I've never done a report before."

"You're kidding. Right?"

"Nope."

"I could help you write yours, if you'd like."

"Okay."

"Meet me at the library tomorrow. It opens at 11:00 on Saturdays."

"Okay," he said.

The bus driver pulled to the side of the road, stopped the big yellow bus, and opened the door. She looked in the big reverse mirror above her head. "This is your stop, Arthur."

What? He didn't want to get off. Not yet. Not until they got to Travis and Tamara's stop. He'd planned to follow them home and retrieve the cloaking device.

The driver turned in her seat. "Come on. I don't have all day. This is your stop."

"I don't want to get off," he said.

"And I don't want to pay taxes. Now get off the bus or I'll have to write you up." She looked out the door and smiled. Her voice morphed friendly. "Hi, Maria. Got your boy here."

Arrth felt a hard shove on his back. It was Travis. "OOOooo, your foster mommy's here to walk you home so you don't get lost."

Left with no other choice, Arrth grabbed his things and got off the bus.

They walked down the long drive to the house.

"How was school?" Maria asked.

"Okay," he said, his mind racing. Already he'd formed a new plan. "Can I go exploring? Check out Willow Creek?"

"I guess so. Don't you want a snack first? I baked a double batch of oatmeal raison cookies with chocolate chips."

A snack sounded good. Lunch was long past and the extra energy couldn't hurt.

"I am kind of hungry," he said.

He sat at the kitchen table and wolfed down only half the cookies. They were really good, and he wanted to eat them all, but he didn't want to look like a warthog. He drained his second glass of milk and stood.

"Those were the best cookies I've had," he said. It was the truth. They were the first cookies he'd ever tasted. Skin-face food was snarfy delicious. "I'm going now."

"Have fun, but be back by five-thirty," she said. "We're having spinach lasagna, garlic bread, and a salad for dinner."

"I will," Arrth lied. He went out the door. By dinner time he'd already have the device and be headed home. Too bad. He'd like to have tried the lasagna.

He pulled the pencil locater from his pocket. He rolled it in his fingers. No point in activating it yet. Not until he got close to the spot where he'd had the positive reading the day before.

Too bad his foster home was so far out of town. He started to run, not fast enough to call attention to himself, but he couldn't afford to waste time walking. Ten minutes later he was jogging up the hill into the main part of town. He stopped at the top in front of the library and stuck the pencil in his mouth.

Nothing yet, just that odd metal taste.

He turned down the first cross street and felt the pencil lead grow warm.

Warmer.

Warmer.

Almost hot.

That's when he saw her—Tamara.

She rode straight at him on two wheels.

He wished he could avoid her, because she made him feel creepy. But that would be stupid.

She was the skin-thief's sister and could lead him to the device.

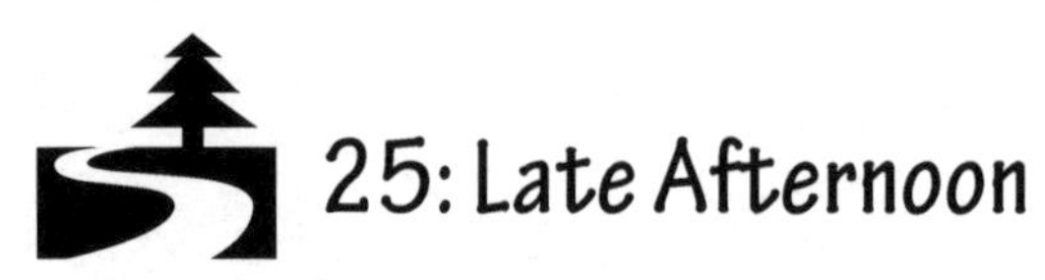

25: Late Afternoon

Four days, three hours until device failure . . .

TAMARA slid to a stop in front of Arrth and straddled the bar that connected the wheels of the contraption she rode.

"Hi, Art," she said and smiled. "You want to ride my bike?"

It would be snarfy, but it looked a little complicated. He didn't really have the time. "No thanks," he mumbled, the pencil still in his mouth.

"Oh," she said in a knowing voice. "You don't know how to ride a bike. It's not that hard once you get the hang of it. I can teach you."

He was temped, wanted to try it, but shook his head. "Maybe some other time."

"What? I can't understand you. Take the pencil out of your mouth. Didn't anyone ever tell you that you can get sick from chewing on pencils? The lead can cause brain damage." She giggled. "I wouldn't want to see that happen to you . . . I'd miss you." She made her lips pout for a moment and then smiled. "I think that's what happened to Travis. You don't want to end up like him." She reached over and pulled the pencil from his mouth.

"Hey," he said and grabbed for it. "I need that."

"I'll give it back if you promise to walk me to Raging Creek for ice cream."

Okay, did he just take it and risk making her mad? But if Travis had the device in their house, he'd have to get inside. It'd be easier if Tamara took him.

"My treat," she said. She swung her leg free from the bike and leaned it up against a fence. "I'll just leave this here and pick it up on the way home."

"Won't someone take it?"

"Come on, let's go. My dad's a deputy sheriff officer and everyone knows this is my bike. No one would dare touch it. He'd lock them up and throw away the key."

Where had he heard that before? He did a quick mind search. Meeker had said it. His mouth went dry. Was her father the police officer he'd met in front of the grocery store?

"Officer?" he said. "Like Deputy Brown."

"That's him. See, even you know who he is and you just got here. I tell you, no one will mess with my bike." She grabbed his arm and pulled him back the way he'd come.

"How far is this ice cream?" he asked, having second thoughts. He didn't want to run into Deputy Brown again.

"Not so far. A three-minute walk. Think you can make it that far?"

He did the calculations in his head. Three minutes there, three minutes back. Just six minutes. Without the pencil it'd take a lot longer to find the house.

"Okay," he said and let her lead him in the opposite direction he wanted to go.

"What's your favorite flavor?" she asked.

"I don't know."

"Mine's mint chocolate chip. I bet you like all of them."

They were on the main street now. Arrth recognized the place where Meeker had nabbed him. She led him to a bright yellow building across the street. The sign on the roof read: Raging Creek Cafe. The place didn't smell like a creek. It smelled like food.

His stomach rumbled.

"Sounds like you need a triple scoop," she said. "I'll order mine while you decide what you want." To the man in the open window, she said, "I'll have a triple. Double chocolate fudge, mint chocolate chip, and cherry chocolate chunk."

Arrth's mouth watered while the man scooped colored ice on top of a cookie cone.

The man handed Tamara her cone. "You, son?"

"I'll have the same."

He watched her nibble at the top scoop. It started to melt and she licked it. He did the same. Only faster.

"Wow!" he said. This was good. He devoured his cone before she even made it through her top scoop.

"I like ice cream," he said. "I could eat a barrel of it."

"You want the rest of mine?"

"If you don't," he said hopefully, forgetting that he didn't like her.

They'd reached the spot where she'd left her bike. She handed him her cone and grabbed her bike.

"This is so snarfy," he said and crammed what was left of her cone into his mouth.

"Arrth, do you have a girlfriend?"

Arrth didn't know what to say. He swallowed and licked his lips.

"Cause if you don't, we could go out." She reached across her bike and grabbed his hand.

He started coughing. "I, uhhh . . . Aren't we already out? Like outside and not inside?"

Her face turned red.

"Can I have my pencil?"

She hopped on her bike. "I thought you were different. Travis was right. You are a jerk. Forget I said anything."

Now what had he done? He wasn't sure, but she sure looked mad. That was not part of his plan.

"I really need it." He smiled, hoping she'd calm down. "You said you'd give it back if I went for ice cream."

"Take it!" she shouted. "And for your information, I saw you talking to Katie. Well, she already has a boyfriend. It's Travis, and he'll kill you if he catches you with her." She tossed the pencil locater into the air.

He reached out to catch it, but missed. It fell between her tires and to his horror she rode over it. Snap.

The ice cream in his stomach churned.

26: 5 PM Early Evening

Four days, two hours until device failure . . .

ARRTH shoved the locater device in his pocket. He couldn't believe it was broken.

What was he going to do now? He thought of his mom, his dad, and Rattles. If the clan had to evacuate, would they let him take the little snake? He doubted it.

He scuffed his feet on the road, disgusted with himself. He'd been so close. It'd been stupid to make Tamara mad.

Maybe if he hurried he could follow her. Figure out which house she and Travis lived in and come back after dark. Hopefully by then he'd have the locater fixed.

He raced to the end of the street where he'd seen her turn.

She'd disappeared. Her bike had vanished, too.

He stood at the crossroad, trying to decide which way to go. Left or right? He looked down. Duh, this was a dirt street. He scanned the ground for the long snakelike tracks the bike would make. There were several criss-crossing one another.

He got down on his knees, bent low, and sniffed the ground. Maybe he could catch her scent.

KAPOW!

Something slammed into him and he landed flat on his back. He blinked and looked up.

Travis leered down at him. He was dressed in full combat gear, spotted camouflage from head to toe. Instead of a gun, a silver box swung from his neck. And he was chewing something. It popped in his mouth and Arrth smelled peppermint.

Travis held the silver box in front of his face and said, “Say cheese.” He pushed a button and light flashed in Arrth’s eyes.

Arrth saw spots. He felt his eyes begin to morph. He turned his head to the side and squeezed them shut.

“Let me get another one of you crying.”

“I’m not crying,” Arrth said between gritted teeth. He got to his feet. “But you will be if you don’t leave me alone.”

“Oooooo. I’m scared.”

“Travis! Dinner time!” shouted a familiar voice.

Arrth turned. Officer Brown stood on the wooden porch of the tall white house on the far corner. Why did the device have to be in the policeman’s house? Oh, well. At least now he knew where it was.

“Next time,” Travis said.

“Next time, what?”

“You’ll see,” the boy said and headed for his house.

“Not if I see you first,” Arrth muttered and brushed dust from his pants. Of course, there wouldn’t be a next time, because in the dead of the night when Travis was sound asleep, he’d come back. He’d grab the device and be gone before they even knew he’d been there.

His stomach rumbled. Midnight was still hours away. He’d go back to Mick and Maria’s and try her spinach lasagna.

He smiled. It was a smart plan.

Retracing his steps, he jogged down the hill and for a second time wished his foster home was closer to town.

He rounded the next corner.

At first he didn’t recognize the maroon-colored car. If he had, he would have gone around the block.

The car was propped up at a funny angle. A big compartment door stood open at its back and blocked his view of someone who rummaged in the rear of the vehicle.

Grunts and groans.

Clinks and clanks.

Thuds and bangs.

“OUCH! Dagnabbit!” Meeker appeared from behind the car. Gasping for breath, he struggled with a round rubber car foot. When he saw Arrth, he dropped his load. It bounced and rolled onto its side.

Meeker grinned. "Perfect timing, Arthur. You can help me change my tire. I'm sure you've had practice," he said and winked. "You look like a budding car thief."

"I'm not a thief. I don't know what you're talking about."

"Sure you do. You can't pull the wool over my eyes. I know more than you think. Now how about some help here." His smile faded. "Or I can tell Maria and Mick about your first day of school. Giving Ms. Hammerhead grief. Starting a food fight."

He handed Arrth a metal cross. "A strong boy like you should have no trouble loosening those lug nuts."

Arrth looked around. He didn't see any nuts. Then he spotted an acorn to the side of the road. He picked it up. "How do I loosen this?"

"Don't try to be funny. You're not cut out for it. Just hurry it up. I have plans tonight and I'm already late."

"Sorry," Arrth said. "I really don't understand what you want me to do."

Meeker huffed. He grabbed the metal cross and demonstrated while he spoke. "This is a lug wrench. It goes on the lug nuts like this. You push down and turn it counter-clockwise until the nut comes loose. Then put the nuts in the hub cap here."

Arrth did exactly what Meeker showed him, except that when he turned the wrench counter-clockwise, the nuts loosened.

Success.

Take the old tire off.

Put new tire on.

Tighten the lug nuts again.

"Put everything into the trunk," Meeker said and got into the driver's seat.

Arrth did it.

"Bring me my coat. It's in the trunk."

Arrth picked up the coat and heard the rustle of a plastic bag. Instantly, his mind transported back to the classroom. Travis holding up the bag of Arrth's fur and Meeker slipping it into his pocket.

Why had Meeker want his fur?

Arrth felt for the bag and pulled it free. Something else fell out at the same time. It hit and bounced off his foot. He looked down. A small flat brown square lay at his feet.

Meeker leapt from the car. "What are you doing with my wallet? I knew you were a thief the moment I laid eyes on you."

He grabbed his coat, the wallet, and the fur.

"I think I'd better have a talk with your foster parents about this."

27: 9 PM Evening

Four days, ten hours until device failure . . .

ARRTH sat on the bed in his room and fiddled with the locater device. He'd fiddled with it for two hours. It still didn't work. The only bright moment in his evening had been the lasagna.

Frustrated, he snapped the pencil into four pieces and threw them at the wall. Useless. Useless. Useless!

There was a knock at the door.

Arrth snatched up the book Ms. Hammerhead had given him and said, "Come in."

Maria opened the door. "Still working? You sure have a lot of homework for your first day. You've been at it since dinner."

"Yeah," Arrth said. "I have to catch up with the rest of the class."

Mick ducked under the doorway. "Get a good night's sleep. Tomorrow we need to discuss Meeker's visit and if you want to stay here with us."

"Mick," Maria snapped. "I thought we agreed not to talk about this until morning."

"We're not talking about it. But Arthur should be thinking about whether or not he's willing to follow the rules. Because if he can't, he doesn't belong here. The boy is supposed to make you happy, not cause problems."

Mick left.

"Have I made you unhappy?" Arrth asked.

"No. That's nonsense," she said and sat next to him. "And you haven't made Mick unhappy, either. He's just under a lot of pressure at work. He's up for a promotion and they want to transfer him to the city."

"Isn't a promotion a good thing?"

She smiled. "You'd think. What's got him down is the city part. He's a small town boy. Willow Creek is almost too big to his liking. So don't you worry about a thing. It's not you." She patted his arm and stood. "It's nice to have someone to bake cookies for."

"I like eating them."

She laughed and then looked serious. "I know we weren't going to talk about it tonight, but you do know that taking Mr. Meeker's wallet was wrong."

"I didn't take it. He asked me to bring him his coat and when I picked it up the wallet fell out. I'm not a thief. You have to believe me."

"I do believe you. Now why don't you go to bed and get some rest. You have all weekend to do your homework. Good night."

"Night."

"And Arthur, we are both glad that you're here." She started to leave and stopped.

"Your pajamas are under the pillow. Hope they're comfy enough for you to sleep in."

She went out and closed his door.

Pajamas? He looked under the pillow. Red, white, and blue stripes. He laughed.

Skin-faces had clothes for everything.

He almost put them on, but there wasn't time to play skin-family. No matter how much he liked Maria and her cookies.

The clock sounded eleven chimes.

Time to go.

He slid open the window. A cool breeze filled the room. Silent and stealthy, he climbed out into the branches of a huge gnarled tree that was older than the house itself. He shimmied three quarters of the way down and then dropped the last ten feet.

He paused and whispered on the night breeze. "Good-bye, Maria. Good-bye, Mick. Thanks for everything."

Night made everything look different.

Black, white, and gray shadows.

Wisps of silent fog floated like ghosts.

Silhouetted trees merged with the black earth.

Except for the occasional dog barking, it was quiet like home. No car engines. Nothing. No skin-creatures out and about. That meant it was safe for him to run at full speed. In ten short minutes he arrived at Tamara and Travis's house.

He paused to catch his breath. He'd already used two days. There was just one left before Uulmer gave the evacuation order. And told his parents where he'd gone.

Think.

The device had to be here. Even though he couldn't look in the house, he could search outside. And if he had to, he could hunt through the house the next day when everyone left. For now, he'd start with the garage.

He stepped onto the lawn, and light flooded the yard.

He froze.

28: 11:00 PM Late Evening

Four days, eight hours until device failure . . .

ARRTH heard a noise made loud by the quiet night. Someone had opened a window overhead.

"What are you doing here?" someone whispered.

Arrth jumped, looked up, and gnashed his teeth. Double worm snot. It was Tamara.

"You've come to apologize. How sweet." Her hand flew to her mouth and she blew him a kiss. "You'd better get out of the light. You don't want my dad to see you."

She ducked inside.

What was he going to do now?

She stuck her head out again. "I have to get dressed. I'll meet you behind the garage."

She disappeared again.

Arrth backed into the shadows. He frowned. Another plan slime-snotted. Still, he couldn't just take off. Not now. She might raise an alarm, and he'd be in a worse predicament.

While he waited, he searched the rocks that lined the edge of the grass. None were the right size or color.

"Arthur."

Tamara stood by the back corner nearest the house. She twirled her finger around a wad of her hair. "I'm glad you came," she said and started toward him.

Her feet must hurt, he thought, because of the way she swayed to-and-fro when she walked. It looked like she'd been hit hard on the head or had snuck some of her father's Bee Mead.

"Your feet okay?" he asked.

She giggled. "You're so funny." She skipped the last few steps and flung her arms around his neck. "I forgive you."

Arrth swallowed, feeling somewhere between unsnarfy and rotten wormy. This was not fair. What was he going to do now?

His fingers clenched and he felt the psychic ring. He smiled. Yes. There was a way out, but this time he'd be extra careful. No foolish mistakes and no foolish thoughts.

He pulled her arms from his neck and held her hands.

She smiled.

Using his thumb, he activated the ring, and stared into her eyes. She closed her eyes, tilted her head, and pushed out her lips like a blow fish. Panic mode kicked in. He held his breath and he began sending her new thoughts.

YOU DON'T LIKE ME. YOU DON'T WANT TO BE MY GIRLFRIEND. YOU DON'T LIKE ME. YOU DON'T WANT TO BE MY GIRLFRIEND. YOU HATE ME!

"Hey, what's going on?" It was Travis.

Arrth dropped her hands.

She stepped back and stared at Arrth like he was a squashed centipede. "I don't like you," she snarled. "I hate you!"

"Sure you don't," Travis said. "I saw you come out to meet this loser. Wait until I tell Dad you were holding hands and kissing."

"Go ahead. Tell on me and I'll tell him that you were out prowling again. Spying."

"Was not. I saw you two from my bedroom window." He laughed and started to chant. "Arthur and Tamara sitting in a tree."

"You can't see this part of the yard from your window," she said. "You had to be outside."

Travis ignored her. "K-I-S-S-I-N-G."

"Stop it," Tamara said. "Or I will tell Dad."

"First comes love, then comes marriage, then comes Tamara pushing a baby carriage." Travis laughed again. "Ouch! Hey, that hurt."

"I'll pinch you again if you don't shut up," she said. "AND for your information, I DON'T like Arthur. I can't stand to even be around him."

The back porch light came on and the door opened.

"What's going on out here?" Officer Brown's deep voice demanded. His shadow stepped out, holding a long gun in both hands. "Come out. Show yourself."

Travis grabbed Tamara's arm. "Come on, Sis. We'll both be in trouble if Dad catches us. We can sneak in the front." He shook his fist at Arrth. "Get out of here and don't come back."

They disappeared around the corner of the garage. Arrth followed, looking for a place to hide, and ran right into a metal can. It fell on its side. Its lid rolled into the street. The stench of rotten garbage filled the air.

Three heavy footsteps pounded down the porch steps, followed by deliberate crunches in the gravel. It happened so fast, there wasn't time to flee. Arrth jumped in a prickly bush and held his breath.

"You chose the wrong house to burgle," Officer Brown said and stepped into the light. He pulled at a lever on the gun. SCHICK! SCHICK! SNAP! "I'm within my legal rights to shoot any intruder that threatens the safety of my family or property."

He pulled something from his waist. Arrth heard another click. A small circle of light instantly appeared and danced across the shadowed grass. He watched in dismay. The beam traced a path back and forth, inching its way toward his hiding place.

Something licked Arrth's hand. His blood turned to ice. It was over. He was about to die.

He looked down. A big white dog licked him again. He flicked his hand, willing it to go away.

The dog whined and then barked.

The light circle flew just inches from Arrth's hand. The dog's eyes glowed red.

"I should have known it was you," Officer Brown said. "Come here, boy. Time to chain you up."

Arrth swallowed. He didn't want to be chained.

The officer patted his leg and whistled. "Duke! Come here."

The dog trotted over to the man. He leaned the long gun against the side of the building and reached down to grab the dog's collar.

"You've got to stay out of my garbage. Or your owners will have to find you a new home."

The deputy continued to lecture the dog and led it to the house next door. He pounded on the front door.

Arrth slipped from his hiding place.

The long-gun changed things. What good would it be if he found the device, but got shot before he could take it back to the valley? It'd be smarter to search during the day when Tamara, Travis, and Deputy Brown were gone.

It looked like he might as well spend one last night at Maria and Mick's.

Back at their house, he scaled up the tree, climbed in the window, and breathed a sigh of relief. It had been a long day and half the night. The soft bed would feel good. He'd even give the pajamas a try. He reached for them and realized someone reclined on the bed.

"Where have you been for the last three hours?" Mick asked, sitting up. "We thought you were in bed."

29: Mid-Morning

Three days, nine hours until device failure . . .

EARLY Saturday morning, Arrth stepped from the hot rain machine and used a bright pink towel to dry off. His thoughts bounced while he tried to formulate the best plan to search Travis's house, but it was almost impossible to concentrate on an empty stomach.

Mist clung to the mirror and morphed his reflection into a hazy memory. He still hadn't gotten used to his monster face, but it wasn't scary anymore. Just different.

He stretched and then squinted. Something in the cloudy reflection looked odd. Under his arms had dark shadows. He wiped the mirror and yelped. Little brown hairs sprouted in both armpits. Sweat beaded on his neck and he started to panic-pant. There was more of it growing on his toes.

"Snarking worm-slimed spider spit."

It was growing in his nether regions, too. Feeling sick instead of hungry, he scrambled into his clothes and slipped on his foot-cloakers.

It was supposed to take six months for his hair to grow back, not five days. Had pushing through the cloaked perimeter changed that, too? There was no knowing how long could he keep up his skin-charade.

Time was running out.

Maybe he should have a few bites of an apple to keep the hair from growing too fast . . . or . . . maybe not. Most skin-faces weren't horrible like he'd imagined, but he didn't want to be one forever. He'd just have to hope there was enough time to find the device before he looked like himself again.

He rushed to his bedroom and grabbed up pieces of the broken pencil locater. Even though it didn't work, he remembered Uulmer's warning. Don't let any Bigfoot technology fall into human hands.

Downstairs in the kitchen, he raided the refrigerator. This might be his last meal for hours. Last night's leftover spinach lasagna rested on the bottom shelf. It tasted just as good cold as it had been hot.

He ate it all. That's when he saw the note on the table.

Arthur,

Help yourself to breakfast. There's cereal in the cupboard, milk in the fridge, and bread in the drawer for toast. Peanut butter on the counter. This is my Eureka grocery shopping day. See ya in a bit.

Maria

The note made him smile for three different reasons. One, the little heart she'd drawn by her name. Two, even though he'd just eaten, peanut butter on toast sounded good. Three, with her gone and Mick at work, he'd be gone before either came home.

Licking peanut butter from his fingers, he grabbed a pencil, and wrote on Maria's note.

Thanx for your helping me.
I won't forget it
or you.

He didn't sign it, but drew a picture of Rattles curled up asleep in a similar shape to the heart. Smiling, assured that he'd done the right thing, he opened the back door. This was the day he'd return home a hero. His smile morphed to a frown.

Mick sat on the back porch, peeling bark off a branch with a little knife. He didn't look up. "Good morning."

"Uhh, hi," Arrth stammered.

"I hope you didn't make any plans for today."

"Kind of. I'm meeting a girl in my class at the library."

"Not after last night. You're on restriction. You're not going anywhere."

Not good, thought Arrth. He had to get out of there. Get the device. "But we have reports due Monday. Katie's going to help me."

Mick studied the wood in his hand, turning it, rubbing his fingers over its grain.

"It's a report on Bigfoot." Then for good measure Arrth added, "I'm not from around here. I don't know anything about them except that they're monsters."

Mick grunted and started to whittle. A tiny bear began to take shape while flakes of wood showered onto the porch.

"We have to go to the library to research. Ms. Hammerhead says we have to have at least three different resources."

Without looking up, Mick said, "You can use the computer in the office."

"Sure. Thanks."

Arrth backed into the kitchen and tiptoed down the hall to the front door. He twisted the knob, careful not to make even the slightest sound. He'd get the device and return to the valley before Mick even knew he'd left. He smiled and eased the door open.

The door flung inward and almost knocked Arrth to his knees.

Mick stood in the doorway. He let go of the door and checked his watch. "Better get started on that report. It's already ten."

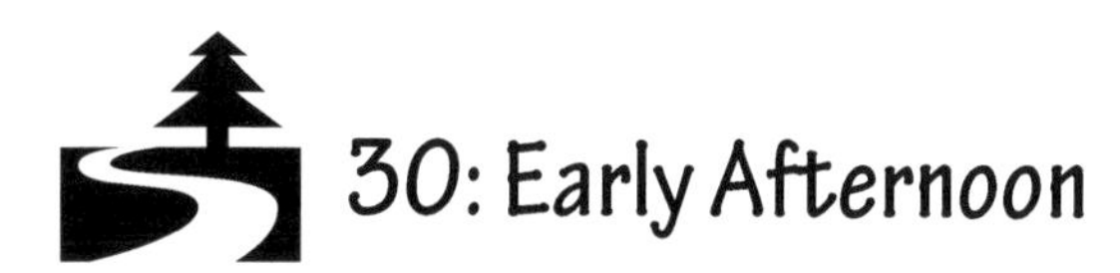

30: Early Afternoon

Three days, six hours until device failure . . .

"Avid-reseacher," Arrth said when he saw the computer on the desk in the house office. "Shouldn't be too hard to figure out."

It wasn't. In twenty minutes he'd vid-surfed at least forty Bigfoot sites.

They were all stupid. Except for the strong, agile, can run thirty-five miles an hour, and are great swimmers, the so-called experts weren't even close to accurate. Worse, they were full of vicious lies. He gritted his teeth in disgust.

Bigfoots did NOT have a putrid, rank odor.

They did NOT eat fish, rodents, dogs, or deer.

They did NOT shriek like mountain lions.

They did NOT leave monumental piles of poop in the forest.

And they were NOT a form of some primitive ape from Asia that came to America on some stupid Ice Age land bridge.

The drawing of the so-called Giantopitheus Extinct Blackie Primate made him frown. It looked no more like a Bigfoot than Rattles looked like a rat. The only thing they had in common with a Bigfoot was hair.

Hair! He'd almost forgotten. He pulled up his shirt and examined his armpit. Had the hair grown longer since that morning? He couldn't be sure. It didn't look longer, but maybe it was.

He'd noticed that some of the boys at school had hairy pits, but knowing that didn't make him feel any better. What if all his hair grew back before he finished his mission? They'd lock him up. Or worse.

"What are you doing? Taking an armpit break?" Mick joked, from the door. What? Mick had a sense of humor.

"No . . . just looking at my new hair." Shoot! Why had he said that? Worse, his voice had squeaked.

"It's a pretty normal thing at your age. Puberty."

Without thinking, Arrth repeated, "Puberty?"

"You know. That time when your body transitions from a boy into a man? You'll experience all sorts of changes. Hairy armpits is just one."

"Yeah, right."

"Finished your report?"

Arrth shook his head. "No."

"Why not?"

"All this stuff is stupid. It sounds made-up."

"What do you mean?"

"They all say Bigfoots are 'primitive' which I guess means stupid. But if they're stupid, how come no one's ever caught one?"

"Good point."

"And if no one's ever caught one, how do they know what they eat? Or any other stuff about them?"

"Another good point."

"Plus, if they're dangerous monsters why aren't the humans scared of them?"

Mick nodded and chuckled.

"The pictures are fakes. And what about the plaster cast footprints? Some have six toes. Others have five. That makes them fakes, too. Right?"

"You're pretty smart. How about I take you on a Bigfoot tour of Willow Creek?"

Mick grabbed the pickup keys from a nail by the back door. "You want to drive to the road?"

"Can I?"

"Why not? You ever driven before?"

Arrth shook his head.

"Well, if you're going to live out here in the country it's about time you did."

"For real?"

Mick tossed him the keys.

After a short lesson about the brakes, gas pedal, and starting it up, they were on their way. Way totally snarfy. Restriction didn't seem so bad. Not that he should forget why he'd come to Willow Creek, but learning to drive might come in handy.

"Wow, this is like being in a live vid, I mean video game," Arrth said. "You just turn the wheel and it goes where you want it to."

Mick laughed. "Stop at the mailbox. I'll drive from here."

They switched places. Mick kept up a running commentary while he drove. He pointed to a yellow and black "WATCH FOR BIGFOOT" sign next to the road.

"There's the Bigfoot Gravel company. The Bigfoot Trailer Park." They drove up the hill to the main part of town. "The Bigfoot Motel. Bigfoot Realty. Bigfoot Beads. Bigfoot Bookstore. And there is Bigfoot."

A redwood carving, sixteen feet tall, stood at the intersection of Highways 299 and 96.

"Looks kind of fat for an agile creature," Arrth said.

Mick turned right and pulled into a parking lot in front of the Bigfoot Museum. Out front stood a huge twenty-five-foot redwood Bigfoot carving. "What about this one?"

"He's better looking."

Mick smiled. "Thanks. I carved it. Do you want to go stand on the brass footprint next to it?"

"That's okay," Arrth said.

"One more stop."

They drove back the way they'd come, but kept going when they reached their turn. Mick drove another block and pulled in front of the Shafer's Ace Hardware Store. It was amazing. The entire wall was covered in a giant mural of humans and Bigfoots working together.

"It's one hundred and sixty-seven feet long and fourteen feet high," Mick said. "So what do you think of Flatmo's vision?"

"Flatmo?"

"The artist. Do you think he got it right?"

"I don't know. At least he didn't make them monsters."

Mick laughed and opened his door. "Come on, I need some nails."

"Nails? What are they for?"

"I have a little job to do."

They were in and out of the store in five minutes. Walking back to the pickup, Arrth fingered a nail. It was like a metal splinter with a flat round top. He wondered how they worked. It didn't look like it was much good for anything.

Mick's cell phone rang. He answered. "Hi, Hon." He listened and his smile turned into a frown.

"What's he want?" Pause. "Okay, we'll be right home."

31: Afternoon

Three days, four hours until device failure . . .

MICK flipped his phone shut and dropped it on the seat between them. He started the pickup and flipped a turn in the middle of the street.

"What's wrong?" Arrth asked.

"Meeker's at the house," Mick said, his mouth turned down into a scowl. "He's got Maria upset."

Arrth felt uneasy. What did Meeker want now?

They made the ten-minute trip in eight. When they arrived, Meeker's maroon car was parked out front, but there was no sign of him or Maria.

"He has no right to enter my house when I'm not there," Mick muttered. He jumped out of the pickup and strode up the back steps.

Arrth followed, feeling a little sick.

Mick stomped into the house and Arrth could feel the man's anger vibrate the floorboards.

"What do you want?" Mick's voice sounded cold, angry, and a bit menacing. "You should have waited in your car until I got here."

Meeker sat at the kitchen table. His pasty face turned even whiter than usual. He'd been drinking coffee and stuffing himself with hot chocolate-chip cookies. His hand jerked like a sudden ten-point earthquake and coffee sloshed onto the table.

"Sorry."

"Don't worry about it," Maria said and put her hand on her husband's arm. "Mick, I invited Mr. Meeker in for coffee while he waited for you to get home. Would you like a cup?"

He shook his head. "Meeker, I thought you didn't work Saturdays.

Why are you here?"

Meeker smiled, showing his gold tooth. Tiny beads of sweat sprung from the creases on his forehead. "Can we talk in private?" He nodded his head to Arrth and winked.

"Arthur, go finish your report," Mick said.

Arrth left the room, but instead of going to the office, he lingered in the hall just out of sight.

"I need to get a sample of Arthur's DNA," Meeker said.

"Why?" Mick said.

"An unidentified man was found dead in a car that ran off the road at Titlow Peak. They didn't find it until this morning. They figure it happened two days ago."

"What does that have to do with Arthur?"

"The man's accident coincides with Arthur's appearance." Pause. "I could tell right away that something was strange about the boy. He seemed confused. Had forgotten things he should know." Pause. "The boy could have amnesia. The dead man could be his father. A DNA test would prove it."

"That sounds a little farfetched."

"You know how government agencies are. They have their regulations and procedures. It's not our place to question their protocols," Meeker said. "I'll just get a swab of his mouth and be gone."

"Not so fast. I don't think that's legal. Do you have an official court order?"

"Not with me, but I will sometime next week."

"Then come back next week," Mick said.

"Don't be unreasonable. I thought you wanted to be a part of the Foster Parent Program." Meeker cleared his throat and started coughing, like a donkey with hiccups. Between brays he said, "You realize the agency avoids placing children with non- cooperative caregivers."

Mick stomped up the stairs. A series of banging thumps followed.

"Here, have a glass of water," Maria said. "Mick's not being uncooperative, he just wants to protect the boy's rights. Isn't that a parent's duty?"

Meeker didn't speak.

"Would you like some cookies to take home? I baked a triple batch," she said.

"You are a kind woman," Meeker said. "So I'll let this go for now. But sooner or later there will be an investigation into Arthur's past. This will just delay it." Pause. "So, how do you like having a child in the house?"

"It's been lovely, but I must confess that for future placements, we'd prefer toddlers or babies. I'm home all day and it seems a waste to have older kids who spend most of their time in school."

"Having a preteen is a bit of challenge, is it?" Meeker said.

Arrth didn't wait for her to answer. He stepped into the kitchen, passed through, and raced up the stairs. At the top, he almost ran into Mick, who was coming back down. The skin-man scowled, but didn't say a word.

That was okay with Arrth. In a few minutes he'd be out of there. All he had to do is to make sure he hadn't left any clues behind. He still had the broken locater in his pocket. Nothing else in the room belonged to him. And he was only taking the clothes he wore because Maria had thrown away his overalls. Still, he took one last look.

Time to go.

He went to the window and pulled up on it. What? It was stuck. He pulled harder. It didn't budge. How odd. It'd been easy to open the night before.

Adjusting his stance to take advantage of his weight, he shoved up hard.

Nothing.

What was wrong? He squinted and frowned. A row of metal dots ran along the length of the window. Where had he seen them before? They looked like the nail heads.

"Worm snot!"

Mick had nailed the window shut. There was no way he could open it without making a lot of noise.

He sat back on the edge of the bed. Time to rethink his escape plan. Maybe tomorrow Mick would have something else to think about and Arrth could just slip away.

32: Evening

Two days, two hours until device failure . . .

SUNDAY *evening* Arrth sat at the dinner table and pushed his food around on his plate. Tonight, he wasn't hungry. The aroma from Maria's cheesy eggplant casserole didn't even tempt him.

All day he'd tried to slip away, but each time Mick appeared just at the crucial moment and ruined Arrth's escape.

Not two or three times, but at least twenty times.

Arrth had the uncomfortable feeling that Mick could read his mind, but that was stupid. Skin-faces didn't have that talent.

He sighed and moved his plate to the side. "Can I be excused?"

"But you've hardly eaten anything," Maria said. "Are you feeling well?"

"I'm fine. I'm just not hungry."

"Maybe I should take your temperature."

"Leave the boy alone," Mick said. "That plate of chocolate chip cookies would have ruined anyone's appetite."

Arrth pushed his chair back from the table.

Upstairs he sat on the bed and thought through his latest plan. Mick and Maria would probably watch their vid-box for at least another couple of hours before they came upstairs. That would give him the time he needed.

The only foreseeable problem was Mick. All day, it was if he'd read Arrth's mind. That meant tonight's escape plan had to be foolproof. He had to take every possible precaution. Think of every possible glitch.

He looked around the bedroom. The window still made the best exit. But, what if Mick checked on him before he got far enough away? An empty bed would be a dead giveaway.

He sat for a long while. Thinking.

Then it hit him. He slapped his knees and jumped up. What a snarfing smart idea.

Arrth ripped back the bedcovers. The chest of drawers in the corner would work perfectly. He pulled out three drawers and laid them in a row along the length of the bed. He frowned. Not high enough. He stacked on a second row. Now it was perfect. He flipped the covers over the drawers and stood back to admire his creation.

"Worm snot."

The hump was too square to pass for a sleeping body. What it needed was padding to round off the corners.

He rolled up the rug and stuffed it in on top. Okay, it didn't look much better, but he'd already wasted enough time. He still had to camouflage the empty space where the rug had laid.

He changed his clothes, tossing the ones he'd worn on the floor. Dropping to his knees, he pulled the tennis shoes from under the bed and flung them into the mix. He couldn't think of anything else.

He'd wait until Mick and Maria went to bed. The bedside clock read 7:00 PM. That meant he'd have about a three-hour wait. Three long, boring hours. Unless . . . He pulled Johnny Tremain from his school bag.

He plopped on the floor, used the bed for a backrest, and started to read. He'd just got to the part where Johnny burned his hand when he heard Maria's voice outside his door.

"Don't sit up too late," she called down the stairs.

"I won't," Mick answered. "I'm just going listen to the weather report."

The bedroom doorknob turned and started to inch open.

Arrth switched off the lamp. "Don't come in," he said. "I'm not dressed."

"Sorry. Just wanted to say goodnight," she said and pulled the door shut. "Don't stay up too late."

"I won't."

The clock now read 10:00 PM. The weather report should be over soon. Then Mick would go to bed. Give them an hour to go to sleep and he could leave.

He turned the light on and picked up the book.

Footsteps on the stairs. Good. Mick was finally going to bed.

The toilet flushed.

Silence.

Arrth watched the clock flip off another thirty minutes.

He went to the door, opened it a crack, and listened. Silence. He crept down the stairs to the kitchen, taking one step at a time. Tiptoed through the kitchen to the downstairs hall.

His stomach rumbled. He shouldn't have skipped dinner. He crossed to the frig and opened the door. The tiny light inside illuminated the room. He grabbed a slab of cornbread and crammed the sweet bread into his mouth. The two pears son the counter went into his pocket.

He inched down the hall. A faint flickering light danced on the hardwood floor of the front room. Too late he realized what it was. Mick sat in his armchair watching a silent vid-screen; men running around chasing a black and white ball.

"Thought you were asleep," Mick said.

"I was thirsty," Arrth said.

"Kitchen's at the other end of the house."

"I know." Arrth felt his eyes morph and looked at his feet. "I saw the light and wondered what it was."

"Just me on guard," Mick said. "You better get back to bed."

Worm snot. Now what was he going to do? The skin-man had to sleep sometime. He'd just wait him out.

"Good night," Mick said, firmly.

"Night," Arrth echoed and returned to his room.

He sat on the floor next to the bed, scowling. Okay, he'd wait another two hours and then leave. He wouldn't make the same mistake twice. This time he'd go out the kitchen door.

He leaned up against the wall and ran through his revised, revised plan. He went over it again. And again. And again. His eyes drooped.

He yawned. His eyes closed. Just for a moment, he told himself. Just for a moment.

33: Morning

One day, eleven hours until device failure . . .

ARRTH heard a noise. His head jerked up. Panic.

Light streamed through the bedroom window. What was he still doing there? He should have been long gone hours ago."Rise and shine," Maria called through the closed door. "Breakfast is on the table. And don't make your bed. Today is wash day."

"Okay," he mumbled and looked at the bed. He started to sweat. What had he been thinking? It looked ridiculous, all square and bumpy. He had to put it back the way it was.

He jumped up, stiff from sleeping on the hard floor. Worm snot! How had he let himself fall asleep? He should already have the device and be on his way back to Bigfoot Valley.

What to do?

He'd have to go to Travis's and hunt for the rock in broad daylight? But what if someone spotted him and call the police? He laughed. Travis's dad was the police.

Plus, there was no guarantee Travis had the cloaking device. Besides, lots of kids smelled like peppermint. And even though the skin-boy bragged about seeing a Bigfoot, no one else believed him, so why should Arrth? Everything was so confusing. His positive I.D. of the skin-thief was fading. So was his foolproof plan to retrieve the device.

And what about the fur? It could have been a dog's.

Still, the evidence against Travis was pretty strong. He had to be the skin-thief. Arrth felt it in his bones.

He bit his lip and chewed. Lately his feelings had been way off. Could he trust them? Not really.

Maybe he should go to school and give it one more try.

Or go home.

He'd already used up the three days, plus one, that Uulmer had allotted. But how could he go home and face the clan without the device? Maybe he could enlist someone to help. But who?

He quickly eliminated the skin-adults. They were too much like clan adults. That left the skin-kids. There was only one he might be able to trust. The skin-girl Katie.

That settled it. He'd go to school. See if he could get her to help him without telling her his real mission.

He raced down the stairs and ate a huge breakfast of pancakes with peanut butter, bananas, and golden raisins. Mick dropped him off at the school just before the first bell.

Katie sat on one of the picnic tables surrounded by a gaggle of girls. He waved, but it she ignored him.

The bell rang. Everyone started toward the classrooms. Arrth hurried to catch up with her.

"Katie," he said. "I have to talk to you."

She went straight to her seat and rummaged in her desk like she hadn't heard him. He took his seat behind. The second bell sounded.

"Katie," he whispered. "Whatever I did, I'm sorry."

"Silence!" Ms. Hammerhead ordered. "Class has started. Pass your reports forward." Pause. "Without talking."

Everyone took out their homework and began passing papers to the front of each row. Arrth quickly scribbled a note on a lined piece of paper and folded it in half before he handed it to Katie.

Travis walked in, a smug smile on his face.

"You're tardy," Ms. Hammerhead said.

"I have an excuse." Travis handed her a pink slip of paper.

"I hope you have your report, too."

"I do."

"Then before you sit down, please pick up the reports, and add yours to the pile."

Travis made a show of snatching the papers. A folded sheet of paper drifted from the stack and floated to the floor.

"What's this?" Travis picked it up and unfolded it. A huge grin flooded his face as he read it aloud. "Meet me at the swings during recess, Arrth. OOOOOooooo. I wonder who this is for?"

"Travis! Sit down," Ms. Hammerhead said.

Arrth stared at his desk. His face blazed and he felt his eyes turn green. He kept them shut until they returned to brown. When he looked up, Tamara stared at him with a bright smile. She fluttered her eyes and mouthed, "I'll be there."

He shifted his gaze to Katie, who had half turned to look back at him. She shook her head.

"The note was for you," he whispered.

"Anything exciting happen this weekend?" Ms. Hammerhead asked.

Katie's hand shot up.

"Katie."

"Around midnight Saturday night I heard noise outside my bedroom window. I let my dog out to chase the intruder away. But all Duke did was sniff up a rat and get into the neighbor's garbage. Now we have to keep him tied."

"That does sound exciting. Anyone else? Travis."

"I took a picture of a Bigfoot."

Everyone started laughing. "Give it a rest," one boy said. "We're tired of your B.F.B.S. stories."

The door opened. Meeker stepped into the classroom.

"Quiet," Ms. Hammerhead said. "Let's have a round of applause for this morning's guest speaker, Mr. Meeker."

A moment of silence, then Katie started to clap, followed by Travis, and then the rest of the class.

Ms. Hammerhead held up her hand. "Mr. Meeker is a member of the Humboldt County Gem and Mineral Society. He is going to tell us about the variety of rocks found in this area."

Travis raised his hand.

"Put your hand down. We can have questions after his talk."

"That's okay," Meeker said. "I'd be happy to take questions as we go. So what's your question, young man?"

"I found a really cool rock up in the mountains. It looks like granite, but it has lots of pale red spots all over it."

Arrth sat up. The cloaking device. He'd been right all along. Travis did have it.

Travis kept talking. "It's really hard. I tried to smash it with a sledge hammer, but I couldn't even chip it."

"That's because," Meeker said, puffing out his chest, "you need a special diamond saw to cut rocks." He made a tent with his fingers in front of his mouth and seemed to be concentrating really hard. "Your rock sounds like a granite boulder embedded with garnets. They're common up near Happy Camp."

"Is it worth any money?" Travis asked.

"Not really. Now, if you'd found a gold nugget, that would be something."

Music blared from Meeker's pocket. He pulled out his mini-talker and looked at it. "Excuse me. I'm sorry. I have to take this. I'll be right back."

He stepped outside.

34: Mid-Morning

One day, nine hours until device failure . . .

THE recess bell rang. Everyone raced for the classroom door.

Arrth tried to catch up with Katie. "Katie, wait up," he said.

She turned and crossed her arms. "Well, what is it?"

"I need your help."

"Like my help on your report?"

What was she talking about now? Then he remembered. He was supposed to meet her on Saturday at the library.

"I wanted to meet you," he said, "but I couldn't. I was on restriction."

"You could have called."

"I don't think you would have heard me. It's a long way from my house to yours."

She rolled her eyes. "On the phone."

"I didn't have your call number. I'm sorry."

"You could have looked it up."

Why did everything have to be so complicated? "I didn't know. If I did, I would have called you. On the phone. I'm sorry. Now are we okay?"

"I guess."

"Good." He smiled. "I need your help. It's important."

"I can help you," Tamara chimed in.

Just what he didn't need; a Tamara complication.

"I need to talk with Katie," he said. "In private."

Tamara tossed her long hair and sighed. "Whatever."

"Hey, Travis," a tall boy shouted and threw a basketball at Tamara's brother. "You sure Meeker isn't your dad? You both like rocks and think Bigfoot is real. You even kind of look like him."

Travis caught the ball and fired it back. The ball hit the boy in the stomach. "Owww. You don't have to get mad."

"You're not funny," Travis said and pulled something from his pocket.

Tamara strode up to the boy and poked him in the chest. "I don't care if you make fun of my twin because he's stupid, but you're treading thin ice when you imply we look like that albino banana slug Meeker."

"I didn't say you look like Meeker."

"You won't be laughing when I'm famous," Travis said and held up a photograph. "It's a real picture of a real Bigfoot. I took it yesterday and e-mailed KVIQ News. They're sending a reporter out tomorrow to interview me."

Everyone crowded around Travis. The photograph made the rounds and everyone had a comment.

"Totally phony," one boy said.

"That the monkey suit you wore for Halloween in second grade," another boy asked.

"You seriously need to get a life."

"Or a pair of glasses."

Someone passed the picture to Katie. She handed it to Arrth. Suddenly he felt weak in the knees and his heartbeat raced to his toes. With his eyes glued to the picture, he pushed closer to Travis.

"Where did you take this?" Arrth asked, keeping his eyes cast down. He knew they were smoking black. "You have to tell me."

"Wouldn't you like to know," Travis said.

"Please?" Arrth tried to memorize every detail of the photograph.

The shape of the hillside.

The pattern of bushes in the clearing.

The trees above the rockslide.

The body trapped under a huge pile of rocks.

The one thing the photo didn't reveal was if the prone Bigfoot still breathed. Please, let him be alive, thought Arrth, touching the glossy picture as if his finger could feel the texture of his father's fur.

He dry swallowed. This was the absolute worst day of his life.

Travis grabbed for the picture.

Arrth pushed Travis away, but held on to the photo. "Tell me where you took this."

The end of recess bell rang. No one moved.

"It's mine, give it to me!" Travis said. He lunged forward, fists swinging.

"What's going on here, boys?" Meeker stepped between them.

Suddenly the playground was deserted, except for Travis, Arrth, and Meeker.

"I'll take that," Meeker said. He studied the photo and rubbed his chin. "Let me escort you boys to class. You don't want to get expelled for fighting." He jingled his change in his pocket. "Art, I hope you realize the favor I'm doing you. You'd better stay out of trouble if you know what's good for you."

"Yes, sir," Arrth mumbled. Meeker was turning out to be his worst obstacle. Why couldn't the man just disappear?

"What about my picture?" Travis said.

"I'll keep it for a little while," Meeker said. He put the photograph in his shirt pocket.

Arrth wanted to rip it from the man's pocket.

They'd reached the classroom. Ms. Hammerhead glared at their tardy arrival.

Meeker gave a yellow-toothed grin and winked. "It's my fault the boys are late. It won't happen again, I promise."

"I hope not," she said. "Or all three of you will have detention."

Meeker's loud chuckle sounded phony, even to Arrth. He felt a hard shove on his back and stumbled into the classroom. The class erupted in laughter, but still he heard Meeker's whispered words to Travis.

"I'll pick you up after school. We'll go get your rock. I'll cut it for you free of charge and you can tell me all about the picture."

Oh no. This couldn't be happening. Did Meeker think the photograph was real?

Arth felt sick.

This whole mess was his fault. If Travis told Meeker where the picture was taken, then the vile skin-man would ruin the clan's last hope of remaining in Bigfoot Valley.

35: Noon

One day, seven hours until device failure . . .

MS. Hammerhead stood at the front of the classroom, writing on the white wall with red, black, and green pens. She'd droned on and on about how a + b = c. And that some combination of x, y, and z could prove it.

Maybe it would have made sense if he'd listened, but all Arrth could think about was his dad's body in the photograph and Uulmer's parting words. That if Arrth didn't return with the device in three days, that Uulmer would tell the clan about the plan.

Everyone would think Arrth's retrieval scheme had failed.

Think he'd been captured.

Think he needed rescuing.

And send someone to do it. His father.

He chewed his cheek. The photograph meant their plan had failed, too. Now it was up to him to rescue his rescuer. To do that, Arrth had to discover where Travis had taken the picture.

One way or another, he'd get it out of the skin-boy. At lunch he'd try the psychic ring on the bully. If that didn't work, he'd stomp it out of him.

Arrth eyed the clock. Come on, bell. Ring.

He closed his eyes for a moment and could see the picture clearly. The hill. The rockslide. The jumble of boulders, almost covering his dad's body.

"Arthur!" Ms. Hammerhead said. "No sleeping in class."

His eyes flew open and he sat straighter.

She went back to writing on the wall.

He wondered if he could slip out without her noticing. No. Bad idea. If he took off now, he'd never know where the photo was taken.

Tamara passed him a folded slip of paper, smiled, and did something funny with her lips. It looked like they were stuck together and trying to escape her face the way they pushed in and out. When they finally unstuck, they smacked like a rock hitting the water.

Katie groaned.

He felt his eyes begin to morph and looked down, but not before he saw Katie's eyes opened wide. Her blue irises totally surrounded by the white of her eyes. If she wasn't careful, her eyes might pop right out of her head.

His focused on his desktop and slipped the note to her without unfolding it.

She opened it, read it, and scribbled something on the bottom. She passed it back with her addition. Now the note read:

Travis took the picture at the old Willow Quarry.
I wouldn't get too excited
No one works there most of the time
so it's the perfect place
for another one of
Travis's fake Bigfoot sightings.
Love and kisses,
Tamara

I can google its exact location on my phone at lunch.
— Katie

He sighed. At least he didn't need to risk using the psychic ring again. The last two times had been disasters. He shook himself. He needed to focus on what to do next. Think!

Okay. The Willow Quarry couldn't be too far from town if Travis had had the time to go there after school on Friday. That meant once Arrth knew its exact location, he'd have plenty of time to do the rescue, and be back to school before the final bell rang to get the rock.

He'd be waiting when Meeker picked up Travis and follow them.

In no time at all he'd snag the device, the photograph, and head home a hero.

The bell rang. Everyone jumped up.

"Sit down," Ms. Hammerhead ordered. "I release you, not the lunch bell." She waited until everyone was in their seat and had stopped complaining before she said, "You may be excused."

Everyone bolted for the door.

Arrth knocked over a desk in his haste.

"Don't even think about leaving before that's cleaned up," Ms. Hammerhead said.

Arrth flipped the desk back on its legs and began stuffing things into it, his eyes smoldering black.

"Neatly. How would you feel if that was your desk?"

Katie nudged him aside and organized the books, papers, and pencils into tidy piles. "Done."

"Good. You may go now," Ms. Hammerhead said.

"Thanks," he said to Katie.

"No problem, I know what it's like to be the new kid."

He raced out the door, rounded the corner, and almost plowed into Travis and Tamara engaged in a serious discussion.

"You're just jealous, Sis," Travis said. "I'm going to be rich and famous."

"Dad won't like it," Tamara said.

"He won't know about it, if you keep your big mouth shut."

"I don't have a big mouth."

"Will twenty dollars keep it sealed?"

Tamara held out her hand.

"I don't have it now. I'll give it to you when I get the reward."

Tamara snorted and stomped off sounding like a wild pig.

Arrth snickered. Maybe it wasn't so bad not having a brother or sister.

Travis turned on Arrth. "What are you looking at? Get lost." Then he stomped off, too, looking and sounding a lot like his sister.

"I've got it," Katie said and snapped her mini-talker shut. "I have the location of the quarry."

"Great," Arrth said. "Where is it?"

"I'll tell you, but first you have to tell me what's going on."

"I don't have time. I thought you were my friend." He started down the drive toward the highway.

Katie grabbed his arm. "Where are you going?"

"I'll find it on my own."

"You can't just leave school during lunch without permission."

"I don't have time for permission." He pulled his arm free and kept walking.

"I saw your eyes change. If you don't stop, I'll tell."

Arrth halted and spun round to face her. "What are you talking about? You think eyes can change? Into what? Ears? Toes? That's stupid."

"That's not what I meant, and you know it."

Arrth bit his lower lip.

"You can tell me, or I can tell Travis. It's your choice," she said.

36: Noon

One day, six and a half hours until device failure...

"LIKE I'd really tell Travis," Katie said and picked a wild daisy from the side of the road leading down from the school to the highway. She started to pull its petals and they dropped like snowflakes on the pavement. "He's such a jerk."

"Then why did you say it?" Arrth said, suddenly feeling awkward.

"I know something weird is going on," she said. "We're friends. I want to help."

"You can help by telling me where the Willow Quarry is. It's a matter of life and death."

"What is?"

Arrth wanted to tell her the truth, but he was afraid. He needed to get moving, but . . . So far everything he'd done by himself had failed. He couldn't afford to fail again. Not with his dad's life at stake. He needed help. Katie's help.

"What's it feel like when your eyes change color?" she asked. "Tell me. I won't tell anyone. I promise."

He swallowed a gulp of air and shrugged. "I don't know. It's like when you bend your fingers or smile. No special feeling, but you know you're doing it."

"Oh." Pause. "Where do you come from?"

Arrth pointed southwest. "My clan has lived there for over two thousand years."

"I thought you came from up there," she said and pointed to the sky.

He half-smiled. "No, that's science fiction."

"If you're not an alien, what are you?"

"A legend."

"In whose mind? Your own?" This time she laughed.

"No. Yours. I don't really look like you. It's just temporary. In a few months I won't look like a skin-face. I'll look normal again, except that I'll have hair instead of fur." Pause. "All over."

"All over? Like everywhere? Your face? Arms? Legs?"

He nodded. "And my feet."

"Then you're . . ."

He nodded again.

"Like the creature in Travis's photo?"

"It's not a creature. It's my dad." His tongue felt thick. "I have to save him."

"I'm sorry. I didn't know the picture was for real. I thought it was one of Travis's photo shopped phonies. What can I do to help?"

"Just give me directions to the quarry. Once I get my dad to safety, I'll be back for that rock Travis is giving to Meeker. It's why I came to Willow Creek. To get it. It's part of our security system. Travis stole it."

A horn blasted and Meeker's maroon car roared up the drive. Arrth and Katie jumped onto the grass shoulder.

"What's he doing here now?" Arrth said and raced back up the drive. "He's not supposed to be back until after school."

Katie hurried to keep up. "What about your dad?"

"I need to know why Meeker came back early."

They slipped behind a big rhododendron bush and watched.

Meeker's car door squeaked open and he got out. Principal Morris walked over to greet him. Meeker talked, waving his hands. The principal listened.

"What are they talking about?" Arrth asked.

"I don't know."

The two men shook hands and disappeared into the cafeteria. A minute later they came out again with Travis. More talk. Then Meeker and Travis got into the car. It roared to life and Meeker shouted out his open window, "It won't take more than ten minutes to pick up the rock. I promise to have him back before the lunch recess is over."

Arrth moaned, his stomach sinking to his toes. This couldn't be happening. Not now. He took off running.

He had to save his father. . . but if Meeker cut the device in two, what would happen to his mother and Rattles?

And all the others in Bigfoot Valley?

It wasn't a real choice. His father would never forgive him if his mother was captured or killed by the skin-faces.

37: Noon

One day, seven hours until device failure . . .

ARRTH crossed the main highway and glanced back at the school. It overlooked the valley a good twenty feet above the 1964 flood line sign. The maroon nose of Meeker's car appeared at the top of the drive.

Nooooo.

He pushed through tall weeds and leapt over the six-foot fence at the side of the road. Crouching low, he looked back.

Katie, her arms flapping, ran out in front of the car. What was she doing?

The car stopped and she ran to the driver's side. Was she going to betray his confidence? Or maybe she was just buying him some time. He hoped so.

What? He couldn't believe it. The next thing, she got into the back seat and the door slammed shut. Meeker's car started moving again.

He didn't know what Katie was up to, but he had to get to Travis's house first. Before Meeker got his hands on the disguised cloaking device.

With a burst of Bigfoot speed, he raced into the Bigfoot Gravel Company and loped through its gravel pit maze of man-made rock mountains. He dodged around them, weaving between the grass-studded pebble piles. Once, twice, three times his feet slipped on the loose rocks, but he kept going.

Meeker's car zoomed past on the highway. Arrth shot back toward the road. By the time he reached it, Meeker's car had already climbed the hill into the main part of town and was turning left.

Too bad there wasn't a quicker route. The long bridge up to the main part of town was the shortcut. At least it was deserted. His feet pounded the pavement and jarred his clenched teeth. In less than a minute, he reached the top of the hill and turned left at the first street, right in front of the library.

Up ahead, Meeker turned left again.

"Faster," Arrth told himself. "Run faster!"

He squeezed his eyes shut and tried to summon more energy. Energy he didn't have.

"Worm snot!"

There's no way he'd get there before Travis gave Meeker the cloaking device. Still, he had to try.

Don't give up. Don't quit.

He had to do this. Uulmer had entrusted him with the future of the clan. His mother and Rattle's future.

His dad needed him, too.

Too late, he saw the pink bubble car backing out of its driveway. He smacked into its side and felt the shiny metal give way before he bounced onto the hard ground. It was like hitting a solid rock cliff head on.

He couldn't breathe. Was he dead?

A dog started barking.

The car door snapped open. The barks grew louder. Seconds later a little dog skittered into view. It yapped and bounced around his head. Footsteps, and then an almost-adult female skin-face stared down at him.

"Oh, nooooo," she cried, almost shrieking. Tears streamed down her face. "I didn't see you. I didn't see you. My dad's going to kill me. Are you all right?"

The little rat dog darted forward and nipped Arrth's ear.

"No, Prince!" She scooped up the vicious little cur in one arm. It squirmed and growled and tried to free itself.

Arrth struggled to sit up.

She dropped to her knees and pushed down on his chest with her free hand. "Don't move. You could have a neck injury. We learned about them in school. In first aid class."

Arrth brushed her hand away. Suddenly he could breathe. "I'm fine. Let me up."

She shook her head and used all her weight to hold him down. Rocks bit into his back. What was wrong with her?

"Get off," he said. "You're hurting me."

Her eyes went wide and she sprang back. Prince wriggled free and dropped to the ground.

Arrth jumped to his feet and took off. Prince chased after him.

"Hey, you can't run away. I have to call 911. You might be hurt."

Arrth didn't answer.

"Prince, come back!"

Arrth stopped, gave the little dog a fierce look, and growled.

The little dog yelped, spun like a dirt devil, and raced back to its master.

Arrth rounded the next turn and stopped, gasping to catch his breath.

Meeker stood at the rear of his parked car. Travis stood next to him, struggling to not drop the cloaking device.

The car's trunk popped opened.

"Set it there," Meeker said. "Push it up near the spare tire so it doesn't roll around."

Travis dropped the rock. It clunked.

"Easy does it, don't want to dent my car."

"Sorry," Travis said. "But it weighs a ton."

Meeker closed the trunk.

"Get in, Let's get this show on the road. We'll go put it on the saw and then head back to school."

It all happened too fast.

They hopped back into the car and drove off. Arrth watched, feeling like an idiot. Why hadn't he rushed them? Taken the device. Done something. Not just stand there and watch the fiasco unwind.

What was he going to do now? He didn't even know where Meeker lived.

"Did you get it?" Katie asked.

Arrth jumped and turned to where she leaned up against the fence. "What were you doing with them?" he asked.

"Told him I had to go home sick."

"Why?"

"I thought if I delayed them, you'd get here first."

"I didn't. Do you know where Meeker lives?"

She nodded and got on her bike. "I'll show you. Take Tamara's bike. It'll be faster. You can return it before she gets home from school."

Tamara's bike leaned up against the garage. He'd never ridden one, but how hard could it be? Probably not much different than driving Mick's old pickup.

And Katie said it would be faster.

It wouldn't be stealing, just borrowing.

He grabbed it by the handles and jumped on.

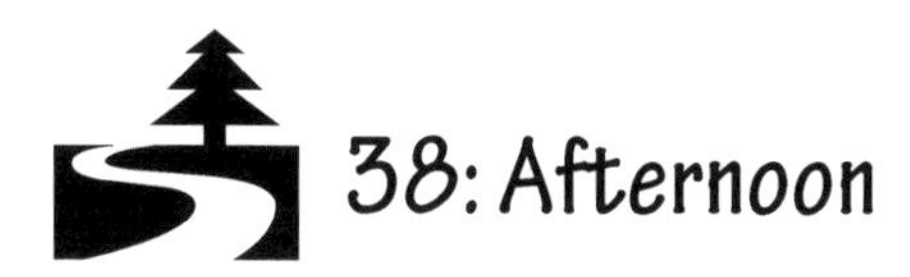

38: Afternoon

One day, six hours until device failure . . .

THIS is a total snarking waste of time," Arrth said and jumped off the borrowed bike. He picked it up and hurled it into a thicket of brambles at the side of the road.

"Arrth! What are you doing?" Katie asked. She stopped and straddled her bike. "I thought we were in a hurry."

"Bikes are stupid. I can run faster."

"Hey, it's not my fault you can't ride a bike."

"Let's not argue. We have to get to Meeker's before he cuts the rock."

Arrth took off running, full speed.

Katie hustled to catch up. She panted and sweat glistened on her brow. "Hey," she said. "How am I supposed to lead when you're in front?"

Arrth didn't answer, but slowed his pace.

"We're almost there." She pointed to a stand of oak trees. "His house is the gray one with the white trim."

Arrth didn't wait for her, but ran on ahead, spurred on by double fears -- the clan's safety and the image of his father's body under the rock pile. Precious minutes had already slipped away. It was time for the direct approach.

Travis stomped out the front door of the house and onto the porch. He was too busy yelling and kicking things to notice Arrth's arrival.

"You can't do this," Travis shouted. "It's my picture, my fur, and my story. And everyone knows it."

"Calm down, boy," Meeker said and followed Travis out. "It's our story. Do you really think anyone would believe a boy? We should be partners. I'll be the front man, and --"

"You'll get all the credit and all the money."

Meeker sighed. "There have been expenses that I'll need to recoup, but we can split what is left, fifty-fifty. That seems fair, doesn't it?"

"No, it's mine. All mine. I did the work."

"Stop and think." Meeker sounded like he was trying to reason with an angry badger. "Who used their own gas to drive the fur sample to the university and paid for its examination? Who's made several long-distance phone calls at their own expense to the media?"

"I already contacted KVIQ news for free on the Internet. I didn't need your expensive long-distance phone calls."

"KVIQ is a nothing little station." Meeker's voice turned hard. "I've made an exclusive deal with The City Sun. They pay real money."

"You had no right to do that," Travis shouted.

"A fifty-fifty partnership is a good deal. You should take it."

"Forget it." Travis sent a vicious kick at a flowerpot full of dried weeds. It tumbled off the porch, onto the sidewalk, and broke into pieces. "Give me back my fur and my photo."

"Your fur? Your photo? I think not. Losers weepers, finders keepers. I found the fur in the trash. As for the photo, I seriously doubt you can prove that it was yours. I posted it on the Internet first."

"But everyone knows the fur and the photo are mine. I showed them to everyone at school," Travis said triumphantly.

"What, some dog hair and my photo you printed from the Internet. You just talked yourself out of a partnership. Now the money will be mine. All mine."

"You should get your rock back, too," Arrth said, startling both of them. "Before he steals it, too."

Meeker stood straighter and stuck out his chin.

Travis said, "Did you hear all that? You're my witness. He's stolen my Bigfoot story."

Arrth shrugged. "I wasn't really listening, but I'll give you twenty dollars for the rock."

"Thirty if it's still in one piece," Katie said.

How long had she been standing next to him, Arrth wondered.

Before Travis could answer, a police siren gave a quick whistle, and a green-striped sheriff cruiser pulled up in front.

Deputy Brown climbed out of his car and walked toward the house.

"What's this, a school field trip?"

Meeker produced a white piece of cloth from his pocket and wiped his brow. He stepped forward and held his hand out to the officer.

"I was just cutting a rock for your son. It's a piece of granite with garnets."

Deputy Brown looked at his wrist. "Shouldn't everyone still be in school?"

Everyone answered at once.

"It's their lunch time," Meeker said. "And I promised to cut Travis's rock."

"Mom gave me permission," Travis said. "And now he's trying to steal my story and sell it himself."

"I went home sick," Katie said, "but then I felt better and went for a bike ride and ended up here."

"I came because I wanted to buy Travis's rock," Arrth said.

Deputy Brown held up his hand. Shaking his head, he said, "Steal? Buy? Sell? How about just one at a time."

Travis's hand shot up. "Dad, he stole my Bigfoot picture. And my Bigfoot fur. And now he's going to sell the story to a magazine and make big money. My money."

Deputy Brown shook his head in disgust. "Not Bigfoot again. Get in the car, Travis." To Meeker he said, "Sorry my kid has been giving you a hard time. I'll take him home and have a little heart-to-heart."

"What about the rock?" Arrth asked.

It was like Deputy Brown didn't hear the question. He looked at Katie. "If you're home sick from school, young lady, you'd better be in bed. Get in the car. I'll take you home, too."

"What about my bike?" she asked.

"I'll put it in the trunk." Now he looked at Arrth. "You need a ride, too? Like back to school?"

"That's okay," Meeker said. "I'll see that he gets there."

Meeker walked Deputy Brown to the car.

Now that it was quiet, Arrth heard the sound of a machine running out back. Was it the rock cutter?

He followed the sound to a small unpainted shed behind the house.

The rock-cutting machine stood alone in the room. He lifted its lid and a spray of oil shot from the machine. He dropped the hood and wiped slick oil from his face.

He spotted a long black cord snaked from the machine and into the wall. The same kind of cord like the one he'd seen on the lamp next to his bed. He yanked on it. The end pulled free and flopped to the ground. At the same time he heard a thunk, from under the hood. The machine ground to a stop.

He threw open the lid and a fine oil mist drifted into the air.

"Nooooooooo," he moaned.

Half of the cloaking device lay on a little platform next to a circular blade. The other half remained clamped into the machine. Hopefully, Uulmer could put it back together.

He grabbed the loose half and tried to pry the other one from the vise. It didn't budge.

"What do you think you're doing?"

Arrth spun to face Meeker. The man's bloated form blocked the doorway.

Meeker held out his hand. "Give that to me. I said I'd deliver the rock to Deputy Brown."

"You can't. It's not Travis's. He sold it to me."

"I don't care. When I make a promise to a law enforcement officer, I keep it. Now hand it over."

Arrth had to get out of there, to rescue his dad and warn the clan.

Well, half the cloaking device was better than none. Arrth pulled the half to his chest, bent low, and rushed forward.

Meeker toppled to the ground. The photograph fell from his pocket. Arrth grabbed it and leaped over the flailing man.

His next stop – the old Willow Quarry.

39: Early Evening

One day, two hours until device failure . . .

THIS has to be the quarry, Arrth thought, but where was his dad?

He held up Travis's photograph and tried to match its pattern of rocks and bushes to the cut-away hillside. It was hard to locate the exact spot, because the quarry stretched way beyond the limited view of the photo.

It didn't show the big yellow scooping machines.

Or the little shack with the "KEEP OUT" sign nailed on its door.

Or that the quarry site wrapped around the side of the hill.

No wonder nothing looked familiar.

He trotted around the rocky curve. A faint metallic scent of dried blood teased the air and grew stronger with every step. Once he'd rounded the bend, he stopped short.

A sharp clenching pain seized his gut, and his heartbeat pounded in his toes. No. No. NO.

At the far side, a flock of huge turkey vultures hopped and fought over a carcass. Pecking and tearing away at the decaying flesh.

Arrth picked up a rock and hurtled it at the scavengers. He rushed forward, shouting and waving his arms.

"Nooooooooooo. Go away. Leave him alone. He's not dead."

The birds took flight, angrily eyeing him while they circled overhead.

He was close enough now to see the bloody remains. So much had been eaten it was hard to tell what it had been in life. Then he saw one inedible, dainty hoof. A deer's hoof. Relief flooded over him. It wasn't his father.

With renewed hope, he returned to his search. The buzzards

circled lower and lower. When he was a good forty feet away, they returned to finish their feast.

That's when he found it. The place in the photograph, but not his dad. It looked like someone had used a scoop machine to shift the rocks and boulders. Had someone uncovered his dad? Saved him so they could sell him to the highest bidder? Someone like Meeker?

The machine had left deep ruts in the dirt. Arrth followed its tracks back to where the three yellow machines parked next to the little shack. The tracks matched the smallest machine.

He examined its scoop. Faint traces of dried blood streaked the metal wall. Bits of dark brown hair caught under a rivet. He pulled a strand and sniffed it.

Yes, his father's body had ridden in the scoop.

He punched his fists together. He should have come here first. What a total snarfing failure his heroics had turned out to be. He only had half of a useless device, and some skin-face had captured his father.

Arrth wanted to cry, but he couldn't. Crying was weak, and he had to be strong. Had to be clear-headed. Think!

He still had one day. There was still time to find his father and get him home. Dead. Or alive.

No. Please, not dead. He could never face his mother again if that were true. He had to believe his father still lived. Otherwise, he might as well go eat a bushel of apples and become a skin-monster forever. Die young.

Think!

Why would someone scoop up his dad? The obvious reason is they wanted to move him and weren't strong enough. The next question, where did they put him? He looked around and then at the ground. A waiting vehicle?

He dropped to his knees and studied the ground.

"Yes!" he shouted.

A second set of tire marks led away from the parked machine. It had parked right under the scoop. He followed the tracks. The gravel gave way to dirt, leaving clear tire impressions in the soft dust. All he had to do is follow them and he'd find his dad.

Wait.

One side of the tracks left a diagonal slash every few feet. It had to be the right rear tire. Good. It would make it easier to identify the right vehicle. He followed the tracks to the paved highway. Faint dirt traces on the pavement revealed that the vehicle had turned left toward town. Then the tracks disappeared. Like his cloaked feet, tires didn't leave tracks on the hard road.

"That's okay," he told himself. "You can do this. Just keep thinking smart."

He jogged slowly and scanned the edge of the road. If the vehicle drove off the pavement, its tread-print would give it away.

40: Evening

One day until device failure . . .

TRACKING the tire prints in Willow Creek proved a lot more complicated than on the dirt lane. Too many paved roads and too many vehicles.

Arrth grew hot, tired, and thirsty. The pavement wore at his feet and they'd started to hurt, but he wasn't giving up. He wouldn't quit his search until he found his father.

Up ahead, water suddenly shot out from a red hydrant. The water spewed into the air with so much force it looked white until it pooled in the road. He headed for it, hoping to cool his toes. "Ahhhh," he sighed and stepped in the pond-sized puddle.

He cupped water in his hand and drank. Sweet. Refreshing. Water.

"Hey kid, get out of the street," shouted a driver who sped through the puddle and splashed water into a rainbow mist. Its tires left clear wet prints on the dry pavement.

Arrth grinned. Problem solved. He'd just sit there and check the tire prints as cars drove in and out of the water.

In fifteen minutes, he eliminated three hundred and fifty-seven cars.

A big shiny red truck drove up and parked. Gold letters printed on the driver's door read: "Willow Creek Fire District." Two men hopped out. They carried big tools. In less than two minutes, the water geyser ended. They got back in their truck and left.

The pond slowly receded to a puddle.

The puddle became damp pavement.

The damp pavement became dry pavement.

Worm snot. No more tire prints, but he wasn't giving up. Time for a car-to-car search.

He went into the grocery store's parking lot. At least he'd only have to check the right rear tire on each car. He frowned. With the cars parked, he couldn't see the bottom of their tires.

Was he strong enough to lift a car and spin their wheels at the same time?

He chose a small car; got on his knees, put his hand above the right rear tire, and pushed up. No luck. He shifted positions. Angled himself and pushed again.

"What are you doing?"

Arrth looked up. "Uhh, hi, Mick."

"I've been looking all over for you. What are you doing?"

"I dropped a five-cent piece. It rolled under this car."

"Forget the nickel. It's time we went home." His foster-dad nodded to the pickup parked in the next row.

"Sure," Arrth said and stood.

"Come on," Mick said. "Let's go. Get in the truck."

Arrth hesitated and then walked slowly around the back of the pickup to stall for time. He pretended to stumble and debated how far he'd get if he ran. He knew he could outpace the skin-man, but not his pickup.

That's why at first, the long diagonal gash ran across the pickup's right rear tire didn't register. He blinked hard to make sure his eyes weren't playing tricks. Then he touched it.

He looked at Mick.

"Come on," Mick said. "Time's a-wasting."

Arrth dry swallowed. His knees suddenly felt weak. He forced himself to get into the truck.

He studied the skin-face's profile. Mick's strong features now seemed frightening. His nose a little over large. The big mouth leering at him.

"Put your seat belt on," Mick said. "I can't afford to get a ticket just now." Pause. "The school called."

Arrth looked at his lap. He felt his eyes morph blue.

"When you live in this world, you have to play by its rules.

Children go to school. They don't just take off when they feel like it. Or take things that don't belong to them."

"Meeker does."

Mick frowned. "We're not talking about Meeker. We're talking about you, Arrth."

A cold tingle raced into Arrth's feet. The monster had called him Arrth. The only way Mick could know his real name was if . . .

What had Mick done to his dad?

"Maria was disappointed she had to leave without saying goodbye."

"Where'd she go?"

"She's gone to Eureka to stay with her sister."

They pulled up in front of the house.

Mick turned off the motor and turned to face Arrth.

"She wanted to take you with her, but I convinced her that you would be better off here with me."

Arrth's skin prickled. He desperately wanted to bolt, but couldn't. Not before he knew what this monster had done to his father.

He twisted the psychic ring, pushed in the red stone, and grabbed Mick's arm. *WHERE HAVE YOU TAKEN MY FATHER?*

He released his grip.

"He's in the basement, but ..." Mick said.

Arrth didn't let him finish. He grabbed the half of the cloaking device and clunked the evil skin-monster on the head.

41: Evening

Nineteen hours until device failure. . .

MICK slumped behind the steering wheel of the pickup.

Arrth wrenched open the door, jumped out, and sprinted to the house.

The front door was locked. He grabbed a chair and smashed out the living room window.

Once inside, he raced to the basement door. Worm snot! It was locked, too. He lunged at the door, pounded it with his shoulder. It didn't budge.

Moans came from under the house. Bigfoot moans. His father's moans.

He crashed into the door again. It held firm. He ran back to the front room and found a heavy fireplace poker.

Through the window, he could see the truck. Mick had sat up. He was getting out. There wasn't much time. He had to move. Fast.

Arrth returned to the basement door and began hacking at it. Wood splintered. The door shuddered and fell from its hinges.

He was through and rushed down the steps, leaping four at a time.

"Dad? It's me. Arrth."

A low moan answered.

"Where are you?"

"Arrth?" His father's voice sounded weak. "Is that you?"

The voice came from behind a makeshift blanket curtain that partitioned off a section of the shadowed room.

Arrth crossed to it and ripped down the curtain.

His father, all seven feet of him, lay on a mattress on the floor.

His feet hung off the end, propped up by three pillows.

Arrth kneeled beside his father. "What happened? What's he done to you?"

His father tried to sit up, but couldn't. "I'll be fine. Did you find the device?"

The overhead light came on.

His father groaned.

Footsteps clumped on the stairs.

Arrth looked over his shoulder and saw Mick at the foot of the stairs. He held the cut half of the cloaking device.

Arrth jumped up. He looked for a weapon and spotted a rack of empty hangers. He grabbed one in each hand and took a position to shield his father.

"Don't, Arrth," his father croaked.

"Stay away," Arrth shouted. "I'm not afraid of you." His voice squeaked on the last word. "I'm warning you. Don't take another step."

He whipped the hangers in the air.

To his chagrin, instead of being frightened, Mick bared his teeth and laughed like a banshee. Then he said the strangest thing, "Beware my bite. If you're not careful I'll chomp off your head and eat your toes for breakfast."

Arrth went slack-jawed. The words sounded eerily familiar. He'd heard them just days ago.

"He won't hurt us," his father said. "He's a friend."

Arrth lowered the hangers, still puzzled. "I don't understand. This doesn't make sense."

Mick held up his right hand, his fingers clenched into a tight ball except for the little one. It stood straight up. "May moss never grow in your brain."

"Or in your ears," Arrth whispered and raised his own little finger to complete the salute. "I must be dreaming."

Mick crossed the room and slapped Arrth on the back. "Don't you recognize me? I'm Taahmic, or I was before I became a skin-face."

"But you're old. It's only been five years."

"That's the price of becoming a skin-face. One Bigfoot year equals six human years."

"So you'll die sooner. Why would you want that?"

"We can talk later. Time is growing short for the clan."

His father tried to sit and started coughing.

Mick handed him a bottle of water. "We have to get you home, Wooodrill. You need medical care that isn't available here."

Arrth's father waved him off. "I'll be fine." To Arrth he said, "Did you get the device?"

"Only half."

"Let me see it."

Mick handed it to Arrth. Arrth handed it to his dad, who examined it, turning it this way and that. He gave a weak smile. "There's still time."

"Cutting it didn't ruin it?" Arrth asked.

"It could have, but the device is in the other half. Do you know where it is?"

Arrth nodded. "And I think I know how to get it."

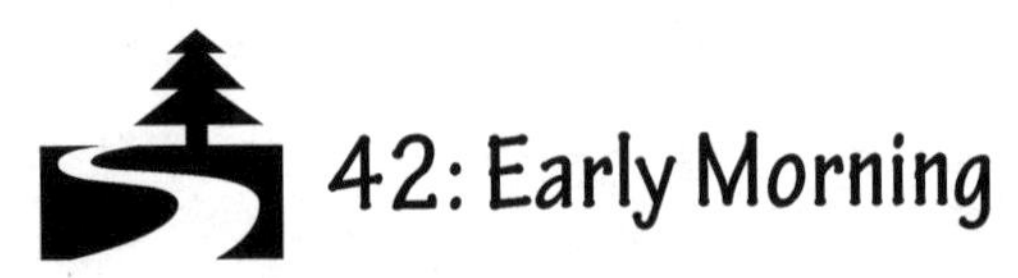

42: Early Morning

Ten hours until device failure . . .

MICK and Arrth sat at a table in Cinnabar Sam's, eating strawberry pancakes and drinking hot chocolate with mounds and mounds of whipped cream.

"You're sure this will work?" Mick asked.

"I'm sure," Arrth said.

"I don't trust that kid."

"On the phone last night, Travis said he'd sell me the rock. He'll meet me at Meeker's at eight this morning. I'll pay him the thirty dollars. He gives me the rock"

Mick counted out thirty one-dollar bills and handed them to Arrth. "You should have offered him ten. He'll probably want more before the deal's done. Here's another twenty."

"Thanks."

"So we're set? But let's go over the plan one more time."

Arrth rolled his eyes. "You sure are fussy since you got old."

"Arrth, don't push me."

"Okay, for the five hundred and seventy-fifth time." He took a gulp of his chocolate and licked his lips. "First we go to Meeker's and get the cloaking device. Then we go back to the house and get Dad. You drive us up behind the quarry and drop us off. From there, it's a short walk home."

Mick nodded. "It's a good plan. Travis is the only weak link."

The waitress stopped by the table. "Anything else?"

"Can I have another order of pancakes?" Arrth asked. "I'm going to need a lot of energy to get through the day."

"Sure, why not," Mick said and laughed. "I'll have another order, too."

When she left, Mick said, "You know, you'll have to apologize to Meeker."

Arrth sighed and rolled his eyes. "If you say so."

Mick laughed.

"Can I ask you something?" Arrth said.

"Sure."

"Why didn't you come back after your *Night Out*?"

"I couldn't."

"Why not? Did you forget and eat some apples?"

Mick smiled. "Yeah, I ate apples. Lots of them! Still do. Every day. Maria makes the best applesauce in the world."

"But why? Didn't the elders tell you what would happen?"

"Yeah, they did."

"But you gave up hunting lizards and snakes, plus four hundred years of life. Why?"

"I fell in love. I couldn't imagine a life without Maria."

"But you'll grow into a skin-faced old-old, and I'll still be young. Don't you miss me and the clan?"

"Sometimes. More at first than now. But fifty years with Maria is worth the sacrifice."

Arrth frowned. "She's really nice and a good cook, but. . . "

The waitress returned with their second breakfast.

"Can you believe all the excitement?" she said. "Willow Creek is going to be on the national news."

"What do you mean?" Mick asked.

"See that table over there?" She pointed. "And that one, and that one?"

Arrth and Mick turned to look at the three crowded tables. The men and women all dressed like Ms. Hammerhead and Principal Morris in matched formal clothes.

"Who are they?" Arrth asked.

"Television reporters."

"Just what we need," Mick muttered. "What's the big story?"

"Bigfoot."

"Bigfoot Days aren't for another couple weeks."

"That's not the big story," she said. "Supposedly, someone has real proof that the creatures exist."

"What kind of proof?" Arrth asked.

She shrugged. "I don't know. But it's good for business." She winked and whispered, "And city folk are big tippers."

43: Morning

Nine hours before device failure . . .

ARRTH and Mick stood on Meeker's front porch. Arrth knocked on the front door. It flew open before Arrth had a chance to step back.

"Oh, it's you," Meeker said, sounding disappointed.

"Art has come to apologize for his behavior yesterday," Mick said. He gave Arrth a little push.

"I'm sorry," Arrth said. He kept his toes crossed and hoped it didn't sound like he was lying. "I'll pay for any damage I did."

"You're lucky," Meeker said. "No damage. I'm sorry, but I'm too busy to talk just now. I have an important appointment."

He started to close the door, but Mick put his hand out and stopped it mid-swing.

"Art also wants to apologize for taking your wallet."

"I didn't take his wallet."

"Art," Mick warned and placed his foot over Arrth's invisible toes.

Arrth's eyes narrowed. "I shouldn't have to apologize for something I didn't do."

Meeker's face flushed red.

Mick's foot bore down on Arrth's toes. "Apologize." He increased the pressure. Arrth's eyes grew huge. "I'm sorry," he finally mumbled.

"You should be," Meeker said. "There's a three strike rule in the foster care system, and you've used yours up. One more little mistake and you'll be headed to juvie."

"Threats aren't necessary," Mick said. "Art's sorry. He won't be causing any more trouble."

"I'll believe it when I see it."

"The second reason we stopped by is to pick up the other half of the rock. Travis is selling it to Art."

"Well, I guess Travis changed his mind. I delivered it to his house yesterday afternoon."

"What a low-down dirt mite," Arrth said when they were back in the truck. "When Travis promised I could pick it up here this morning, he already had it at his house."

"I told you I didn't trust him. "

"Can you take me to his house?"

Mick's mini-talker rang. He listened for a few minutes and stuck it back in his pocket.

"I'll drop you there. I have to run into work even though they gave me the morning off. It seems that this media circus is disrupting all sorts of things. You get the rock and I'll meet you back at the house by noon at the latest."

Arrth hopped out of the truck. He watched it drive away and steeled himself for his confrontation with Travis.

The skin-boy must have expected him. He came out onto the front porch before Arrth even entered the yard.

"Got my money?" Travis asked.

"I went to Meeker's this morning. Where's the rock?"

"I did some thinking. It must be worth more than thirty bucks if you want it so bad. The price just went up."

"But we had a deal."

"You want the rock?"

"Yeah."

"Then give me fifty bucks and you can have it."

"NO. First, you give me the rock."

Travis laughed and shook his head. "Not on your life. You know, there's something about you I don't trust. Since you turned up last week, all sorts of weird things have happened."

Arrth clenched his toes. "You promised to sell me that rock."

"Okay. I'll sell you the lousy rock, but . . ."

"But what?"

"First you have to do something for me," Travis said with a smile.

44: Morning

Eight hours until device failure . . .

"YOU'VE *got to* be kidding," Arrth said after Travis told him what he wanted done. "It's a stupid idea."

"That's the deal," Travis said. "The reporter will be here in a few hours."

"Can't you get one of your friends to do it?"

"The whole point is to convince them I've been telling the truth."

"So you don't care about the money."

"I didn't say that," Travis said. "I'm just tired of everyone thinking I'm a dorknoid. Even my dad doesn't believe me. He thinks I made the whole thing up. I didn't. I saw a Bigfoot." Pause. "I touched it."

"A real Bigfoot," Arrth said, but thought, you forgot about the part where you bit me. What he said is, "You sound like Meeker."

"Do you want the rock or not?"

"How do I know you won't change the deal again once I've done it?"

"I won't. If you do this, I promise, I'll give you the rock."

"How about this?" Arrth said. "I give Katie the money. You give her the rock. I do the deed. She gives you the money."

Travis kicked at the grass. He ran his hand over the tops of the picket fence. Finally he said, "Okay, but it has to go down at exactly the right time. You got a watch?"

Arrth shook his head.

"Here take mine," Travis slipped his off. "I've got a spare. You know where Willow Creek runs into the Trinity River? It's right there at Big Rock, next to the gravel piles."

"Yeah. I know where it's at."

"There's a little sandbar. That's where you leave the prints. And you need to be suited up by 10:30 a.m. You can tell time, can't you?"

"I'm not stupid."

"I'll bring the reporter at 10:45 a.m. Once I've shown her the tracks, I'll drop my hat in the river. That's when you jump out. Make sure she sees you. Then run up the hill, and stay in the open. Got it?"

"Got it."

"One last thing," Travis said. "Here's my cell phone. Call Katie when you reach the top. She'll have the rock."

"Okay."

"Wait here, while I go get the stuff you need to pull this off." Travis went to the garage and came out lugging two poles, duct-taped onto a big, fluffy black plastic bag. "You'll need these for the sand."

Travis handed Arrth the cumbersome poles.

"I doubt you can carry the poles while you're running. Hide them good. I don't want anyone to find them. You can return them when all the reporters are gone. I'm trusting you."

"No problem. I'll take care of it," Arrth lied. He planned on being gone long before the reporters and television crews left Willow Creek.

"Why are you making me do this?" Arrth said.

"Do you know what it's like to be called a liar all the time? I just want a little respect."

"Then don't always act like such a termite."

"Termite?" Travis frowned. "And people think I'm weird."

"This won't change things."

"Maybe not, but Meeker's not stealing my story without a fight. Now get going. You have one and half hours to get this set up."

"What if someone sees me?"

"Don't let them."

"Haven't you seen all the television crews in town?"

"What are you talking about?"

"They're all over. We could get caught."

Travis frowned, then shook his head. "I don't care. It's too late to back down now. Just make sure you place those prints about six feet apart. With the right on the right, and the left on the left. Got it?"

"Sure thing. Right on right. Left on left. Six feet apart."

45: Mid-Morning

Seven hours, forty-five minutes until device failure . . .

THE street looked deserted. Travis had gone back inside his house.

No use standing around, Arrth thought. The way his luck had been going, Tamara or Deputy Brown would probably come out and grill him.

He hoisted the two long poles to his shoulder; the lumpy black bag dangled on his back. How totally snarking awkward. Worse, the plastic made his neck sweat, and the accompanying "crackle, crackle, crackle," almost drove him crazy.

AND the poles kept slipping.

He rounded the corner, stopped in front of an empty field and looked around. Good. None of the houses faced this direction. Time to unload. He swung the bag off his shoulder and plopped it on the ground. Why carry all this junk down to the river when all he really needed was the suit.

He picked at the silver tape that bound the bag to the poles without success. The tape stuck like hardened pitch. Annoyed, he ripped the plastic bag from the poles.

That's when he got his first look at Travis's great invention. On the bottom of each pole he'd attached a giant foot carved out of wood.

Arrth laughed.

If Travis only knew. . . Arrth didn't need fake feet to plant giant footprints in the sand.

He lobbed both poles into the tall yellowed grass and bundled the foot molds into what was left of the bag. He had plenty of time, but he still had to give Katie the money and tell her the new plan.

He pulled out the mini-talker, pushed a button, and held it to his ear. "Call Katie," he said. And waited.

"Quit calling me, Travis," Katie's voice said. "I'm hanging up."

"Wait. It's not Travis. It's me."

"Arrth? What are you doing with Travis's phone?"

"How do you know it's his?"

"It's on the display."

"Oh . . . Have you talked to Travis this morning?"

"No. After yesterday I'm never talking to him again."

"You'll have to. I made a deal to get the second half of the rock. It won't work without your help."

"You can't trust him, he's –"

"Just listen. I'm around the corner in the little field by the hill. Ride your bike over here and I'll explain."

"I'm not dressed yet."

"Then get dressed. But make it quick."

"You're starting to sound like Travis."

"Sorry. Please hurry, I only have about fifteen minutes."

"Okay."

He flipped the mini-talker shut and waited, pacing up and down the road. A pink car pulled up alongside him.

"Hey, kid, you still okay?" It was the teenage girl who backed into him yesterday. "I still think you should go to the doctor and get checked out."

"I'm fine," Arrth said.

"If you say so, then I guess I don't have to tell my parents." She smiled, showing off big white teeth, and tossed her hair. "Besides, I've realized it wasn't my fault. I didn't run into you. You ran into me."

"Yeah," Arrth said, wishing she'd just leave.

"I saw you throw that trash in the weeds. You shouldn't do things like that; it's bad for the environment. We learned all about that in my civics class. Just think if everyone threw out their trash on the road. It'd get piled so high you wouldn't see the trees."

"Yeah."

"Aren't you going to pick it up?"

"Sure," Arrth said, and retrieved the black plastic bag he'd set down when he called Katie.

The female's smile grew even wider. "Now don't you feel better already, knowing that you're helping to save the environment? I know I do."

She didn't wait for his answer, but sped down the road, almost hitting Katie coming along on her bike.

"You okay?" Arrth asked.

"I'm fine," Katie said. "Now what's the big rush?"

He pulled out the money Mick had given him and handed it to Katie.

"What's this for?"

"Give it toTravis after he gives you the rock."

She was counting the money. "No rock is worth fifty dollars."

"Just give it to him. Once you have the rock, call me. We'll meet at the library."

"Why don't you give him the money yourself and let him give you the rock?"

"The money is just part of the deal. I have to do something for him, too."

"What?"

"Can't tell you."

"Why not?"

"That's part of the deal."

"I wouldn't trust him."

"I have to. I have no choice. Will you help?"

"Of course."

"Thanks, I've got to go."

"Will I see you again?"

He shrugged. "I'm not sure. Maybe, it depends on how this goes down."

She looked worried. To his surprise, she stepped closer and brushed her lips on his cheek. It happened in an instant and she had already stepped back, hopped on her bike, and was pedaling back the way she'd come.

His hand went to his face. It felt like a butterfly had brushed his skin and flitted away.

Not at all like one of his mother's kisses. More like a honey snarf. Is this how Mick felt when he'd met Maria?

He shook off the unbidden thoughts. There wasn't time. Not now. He'd think about it later. Now he had to get moving.

Clutching the plastic bag close to his chest, he jogged toward Big Rock.

46: Morning

Five hours, thirty minutes until device failure . . .

ARRTH sat on a drift log left high and dry from last year's high water. The river was still low. It would be another couple of months before the rains began. The log had been lodged in the bushes twenty feet from the water's edge. The bulging black plastic bag sat at his feet.

He sighed. Katie should have called on the mini-talker by now. What was the holdup? Hadn't Travis given her the rock yet? He wouldn't put Travis's plan into motion until she had the cloaking device.

Overhead, big fluffy clouds dotted the blue sky. An osprey called to its mate while it soared overhead. Arrth liked the smell of the river.

He looked at the watch on his wrist, and frowned. It'd only been five minutes since he'd last checked. Why did it feel like hours? He got up and started to pace. Maybe he should call Katie.

He pulled the mini-talker from his pocket and pushed a button. Nothing. He pushed another. Why had the stupid thing stopped working? It was worthless. He threw it down on the sand. It landed and started blaring music.

He snatched up the phone and held it to his ear.

"Hello?"

It continued to blast music. He pushed a button. Another button. And another. The music stopped. He held the talker to his ear. "Katie?"

"No, it's me," said Travis's voice. "Have you finished phase one?"

"Have you given Katie the rock?"

"If you don't do it soon," Travis said, "it'll be too late."

"Yeah, so give her the rock. Or do you want to show the reporter an empty river bar?"

"Okay. Bye."

Arrth looked at the watch again. Another five minutes passed before the talker blared music again. This time he remembered which button to push. "What now, Travis?"

"No, it's me, Katie. I've got the rock."

"Good. Take it and hide it, but don't let Travis see you do it. I'll get it from you on my way out of town."

"Okay." Pause. "Good luck."

"Thanks. I'll need it."

No time to waste. He slipped off his foot-cloakers, stuffed them into his front pocket, and wiggled his toes. He laughed. His feet looked gynormous after not seeing them for five days.

He smiled. His feet would leave better imprints than Travis's fake carved wooden ones.

He gathered the bulky bag into his arms and started running toward the spot where the Willow Creek flowed into the Trinity River. He leaped from one foot to the other, spacing out his prints. He laughed. How did Travis know he had a six-foot stride? His dad's stride was eight feet.

The prints weren't very distinct in the soft dry sand. He wondered if Travis had thought about that.

Arrth felt an unexpected pity for the obnoxious skin-boy. Surrounded by tons of kids, he was more alone than Arrth had been in the valley. Arrth bopped his head. What was he thinking?

If Travis stopped acting like a jerk, he'd have lots of friends.

Still, a deal was a deal. Katie already had the rock, and he'd agreed to leave tracks for Travis to show the reporter. Near the river's edge, the damp sand would hold better impressions.

He ran along the water's edge, leaving three good prints, and then hopped onto a graveled section. He crossed Willow Creek and moved into the bushes to wait for Travis and the reporter. He looked at the watch one more time. Twenty minutes before they'd arrived, but how long would it take to get suited up?

He pulled the black furred costume from the bag. A musty odor clung to it. Gross. It had creases, cobwebs, and moldy dust. He shook the big, one-piece cloth skin and cringed when he slipped it on over his clothes. He breathed through his mouth. Travis could have at least washed it.

One last thing to go on, the head. He frowned. Its gorilla face didn't look at all like a Bigfoot. If it could fool the newspaper gal, then she must be pretty stupid.

Arrth sniffed. Ewwe. He shook it. Little rat droppings fell through the plastic eye sockets. Triple, quadruple, disgusting worm snot!

There was no way he was putting it on his head.

But he had to. A deal was a deal.

He returned to the stream and dunked the gorilla head into the water. He swirled it a couple of times and pulled it out. His mother would be proud, he thought, and wrung most of the water from it. He'd wait until the last minute to put it on.

Then came the sound of a car pulling into the parking lot on the hill overlooking the river bar. Doors opened and closed. Voices drifted toward him on the breeze. A man's, a woman's, and Travis's.

Showtime.

Giving the gorilla head one last shake, he slipped it on over his head.

47: Noon

Three hours, eight minutes until device failure . . .

ARRTH crouched low while he stared through a tiny break in the willow clump, his view framed by the black eye sockets of the gorilla mask. At least fifty paces separated him from Travis and the two reporters. The distance, coupled with the head covering, muffled most of their words, but Arrth could pretty much guess what Travis was saying.

"Look, here's a Bigfoot print!" Travis pointed. "There's another. And another."

The man started taking pictures, while the woman wrote notes and asked questions.

Talk. Talk. Talk.

Hurry it up. The suit was getting hot and his skin started to itch. Plus it smelled like rat pee. Sweat trickles began to crawl down his neck. He shivered in spite of the suffocating heat.

Come on. Let's get this over with. Give the signal, Travis. Drop your hat.

Now what was Travis doing? Why was he taking off his shoe and rolling up his pant leg?

The man reporter nodded and smiled. He pointed to a sand imprint and Travis placed his foot next to the Bigfoot print. The man snapped two more pictures.

More talk.

More note taking.

Arrth had waited long enough. He stood, stretched his cramped muscles, and stepped from his hiding place.

Not one of the three even noticed him.

Disgusted, he picked up a tiny pebble and aimed it at Travis's back. It soared through the air and found its mark. Travis yelped.

Arrth laughed and then let out a wild roar. He threw three more fist-sized rocks, all carefully aimed to miss.

The three on the beach turned to stare at him.

The woman's hand flew to her mouth but failed to hold back a high-pitched shriek. Her eyes glowed bright with excited fear.

The man jerked the camera to his face.

Travis didn't say anything, but he grabbed his hat and flung it on the ground. An angry tight frown distorted his face.

Arrth lobbed two more melon-shaped rocks and took off. He pushed through bushes and made for the pyramid-shaped hill just ahead. It was steep and covered in fir, madrone, and pine trees interspersed with stunted vegetation sprouting from patches of the hard, rocky soil. If he could get to the top and shed the costume, he could slip back into town and retrieve the cloaking device.

The gorilla suit made climbing awkward, and he was forced to slow while he scaled upward, using the trees and brush for handholds to pull him higher. And higher.

Below, shouts erupted from excited spectators.

From the road to his right came the screech of tires and several horn blasts. He looked. Several cars had stopped on the raised bridge connecting the low plain to the main part of town. Drivers got out and stood in the middle of the road, pointing in his direction.

More shouts.

He glanced down. Where had all the people come from? There were at least a dozen men climbing the hill below him.

Arrth scrambled faster. He aimed for the dense brush thicket at the top where he could lose the gorilla suit. He put on a burst of energy, lunged upward, and fell back. His right leg snared.

"Worm snot!"

The bulky costume had caught on a branch. He thrashed and tried to roll his leg free, but it held tight.

Below, the man in the lead narrowed the gap between them. If Arrth didn't get moving, the man would catch up, and everything would be lost. His mother and father's safety. The cloaking device.

Bigfoot Valley.

He roared.

Reached down.

Grabbed the branch.

Using every bit of strength, he yanked up on it. At the same time he kicked out with his foot.

A shower of pebbles raced down the cliff-face. The man yelled.

Arrth kicked again. This time his effort was rewarded.

Riiiiiippp! The faux fur tore from his knee to his ankle. It flapped while he scuttled over the rocky soil and dense weeds.

Almost there.

Just another ten feet to go.

48: Afternoon

Two hours, fifty-five minutes until device failure . . .

ARRTH stood on top of the hill, panting to catch his breath. He raised his arms and shook both fists high in the air. He'd made it!

It felt so good that he decided to give Travis a bonus on their deal. He turned and looked down at the men climbing towards him.

"ARRRRRRRRRRR," he howled.

Laughing, he slipped into the woods. The wooded pyramid mountain had been a genius escape route. Even though it stood right in the middle of town, no one lived on it. Which was a little odd, because it took up more room than the town itself. If he lived in Willow Creek, he'd want his house on the tip-top.

Of course, he didn't live in Willow Creek. He lived in Bigfoot Valley, and he'd better get moving. He had less than three hours to get the cloaking device, rendezvous with Mick and his father, and make it back to the valley.

He quickly shed the gorilla suit. It felt good to have it off, even if now he smelled like rat pee. At least his skin could breathe. There was no way he was lugging the stinking thing back to town.

An ancient red-barked madrone tree caught his eye. It stood majestically overlooking the town below like a sage guardian. It'd be perfect for what he had in mind.

Travis had wanted him to make the footprints, wear the gorilla suit, and climb the hill in plain sight of the reporters. He'd done all that. Plus he'd handed over the money.

The cloaking device was paid for in full.

That meant he was free to do what he wanted. Laughing, he

picked up the suit and climbed the madrone. It was a good forty feet tall. At the top he secured the suit to the branches with his belt. The headless costume fluttered on the breeze. He stuffed the gorilla head over the end of another short limb and pulled it down close to the trunk. The stubby limb stuck out through the eye.

He climbed back down.

On the ground, if you stood in just the right place, it looked like the head was attached to the body.

Voices drifted on the breeze from the Big Rock side of the mountain. Time to go.

He called Katie on the mini-talker. "I'm coming down."

"I'll be there."

Running down the hill took less time than climbing up had. In no time at all he reached the road. Katie should be in the library parking lot just a block away.

He spotted her leaning against an oak tree near the back of the building. His stomach lurched. Where was the cloaking device? She was supposed to bring it.

"Where's the rock?" he asked, afraid that something had happened to it.

"Hi to you, too." She slipped off a green and black backpack and handed it to him. "I thought it'd be easier for you carry in this."

"Thanks." He put on the pack.

A loud whoop, whoop, whoop sounded overhead. He looked up. In the sky, a giant flying machine hovered above the mountain top. "What's that?"

"A helicopter."

"What's it doing there?"

"See the letters, KVIQ News? It's probably looking for you. Good thing you're here." Her smile morphed and a strange expression stole over her face.

"What's wrong?" he asked.

"Your feet."

Shoot. He'd forgotten about the foot-cloakers. He looked down and wiggled his toes. "Like my real feet?"

"They're big . . . "

"You should see them hairy," he said. "Makes them look even bigger."

"Arrth!" called a familiar voice.

Arrth and Katie turned.

"Oh, no," he said. "What's she doing here?"

"I don't know, but you'd better not let Tamara see your feet."

"Wait up," Tamara called, and she rushed towards them. She carried a stack of books.

Frantically he dug in his pockets for the foot-cloaker bands.

"Hurry," Katie urged and moved to shield him from Tamara's view.

He slipped one band on and dropped the other. "Worm snot!" he said while the second band rolled into the ditch. This was not good. A sudden whoosh of water cascaded down the ditch like a flash flood. OH, NO. The cloaker was carried away in the rush of muddy water. This was a hundred times worse than not good.

He looked at his feet. One foot had shrunk into a running shoe. The other was bare and gigantic, at least twice the size. If Tamara saw it, she'd have a serious snarf fit.

He nudged Katie. "Delay her."

"How? She doesn't want to see me. She wants to see you."

"I don't know. Just do something. I have to get the other cloaker."

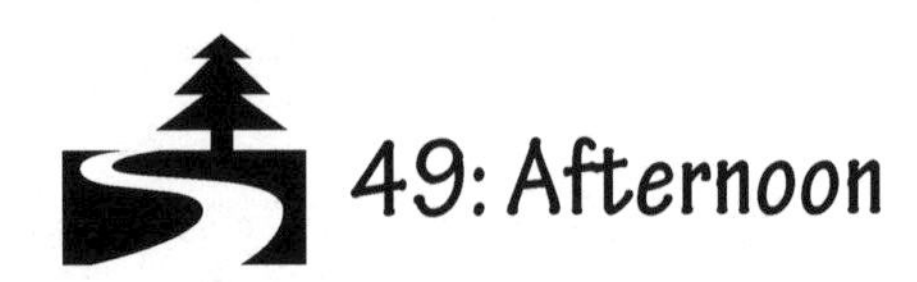

49: Afternoon

Two hours, thirteen minutes until device failure . . .

TAMARA pushed past Katie and headed straight for Arrth.

"Hi, Arrth," Tamara said and flashed him a big smile. "Why are you standing in the ditch water?"

"My feet are hot," he said and hoped Tamara couldn't see his real foot in the muddy water. He motioned with his eyes for Katie to retrieve the foot-cloaker floating farther and farther away.

Katie didn't catch the hint.

Tamara laughed. "You're so funny." She looked at Katie. "If you don't mind, I need to talk to Arrth. In private."

"Give us a minute," he said to Katie and pointed toward the cloaker almost a full block away.

At first Katie frowned, but then she smiled. "Sure thing."

Katie jogged down and grabbed the foot-cloaker. He sighed when she held it up, but then she slipped it over her wrist. Instantly her hand transformed into a running shoe. She pulled it off, but the look on her face made him laugh.

Tamara giggled, not taking her eyes from his face. "I'm a little nervous, too. Let's go over there." She pointed to a bench.

"My feet are really hot. Let's talk here."

"Okay."

"So what do you want to talk about?"

She smiled and fluttered her eyelashes, then grabbed his hand. "I want to be your girlfriend. Your exclusive girlfriend."

"Exclusive?"

"Yeah. We could spend all our time together, holding hands or . . ." She winked and did something funny with her lips. "Of course, you'll have to quit hanging out with Katie."

"Can't a person have more than one friend?"

"Not if he's my boyfriend."

"Oooohh," Katie interrupted. "So you have another new boyfriend?" The cloaker-band dangled from her finger. She dropped the band in the water and it hit his foot.

"No one asked you," Tamara said, looking angry.

He stepped on the band before it could float away again. He bent down, slipped it on, and stepped out of the water. Now his feet looked like a matched pair of very wet running shoes.

"Katie, be nice," he warned.

Tamara's eyes narrowed. "Hey. Isn't that Travis's watch?"

"Yeah, he let me borrow it." He took it off and handed it to her. "I have to get home. Can you give it back to him for me?"

"He doesn't let people borrow his things."

"Well, he did this time," Katie said.

50: Afternoon

Two hours, one minute until device failure . . .

ALONE at last and female free, Arrth stood in front of the library and looked down the raised roadway to the plain that stretched across the river valley. A lone red-tailed hawk swooped down and hit the grass at the side of the pavement. Seconds later, it lifted into the air. Trapped in its claws, a small rodent wriggled helplessly. Poor thing. Doomed to die.

He knew how it felt.

He had to get back to Mick's place. Fast. In just two hours the entire cloaked perimeter of Bigfoot Valley would fail if the cloaking device was not back in its place.

Just stick to the plan, he told himself.

Get back to Mick's.

Get his dad.

Go home.

Still, he couldn't afford one more mishap or any more foolish delays. Not now. Not when he had the device and his father needed medical treatment.

Down below, parked cars, vans, and pickup trucks still lined both edges of the road. It seemed like everyone in town was there, hoping to catch sight of Travis's Bigfoot. The pyramid mountain blocked his view of the river bar, but he could imagine the crowd of skin-faces gathered on the beach.

Did he dare jog down the road, past all the parked vehicles? What if someone saw him? Plus he had go past the school, too. If Ms. Hammerhead, Meeker, or the school principal spotted him, it was over.

There had to be another way. A faster way.

What he needed was a car. A car with a driver, and he knew just the person. "Let her be home," he chanted while he ran.

He rounded the corner and smiled. The little pink bubble car sat parked in the driveway of the brown house. He ran to the front door and pounded on it. Loud barks erupted from the other side of the door. It sounded like there were at least a dozen angry dogs locked inside.

The door opened.

"Oh. It's you," the teenage skin-face girl said. She held her little dog, Prince. It bared its teeth and growled. "Does your head hurt? You should have let me take you to the medical center yesterday. You could have a concussion, but maybe not. I mean, if you went to sleep last night and woke up this morning, you probably don't. Or you'd be dead or in a coma instead of standing at my front door." She paused to breathe.

Prince started barking.

"I need a ride," he shouted.

"Shhh, Prince." She put the dog inside, stepped outside, and quickly shut the door. "My mom said I'm not a taxi service. That I can't give rides to my friends. Besides, it's against the law. I learned all about it in Driver's Ed. There has to be an adult in the car if my passengers are under eighteen or I'll lose my license."

"No problem. I'm seventy-seven-and-a-half."

She giggled. "You're so funny."

"Seriously, I need a ride. Now."

"I can't. My parents would kill me if I got a ticket the first week I had my license. They'd take it away. I wouldn't be able to drive until I was eighteen."

"How would they feel about you backing into me? Or did you tell them about that?"

Her skin paled under its face paint. "You wouldn't."

"It's up to you."

She looked worried. "Okay, but just this once if you promise then we're even."

He nodded.

She ran into the house. Seconds later she returned, jingling her keys. "Get in and scrunch down. That way no one will see you."

Arrth hopped in. Instead of starting the car, she lowered a mirror and rubbed red stuff from a tube on her lips.

"What are you doing?" he asked.

"I have to look my best when I'm driving. It's a confidence thing. According to TEEN magazine, self-image is everything."

"I'm in a hurry."

She made an impatient "tisk tisk" sound with her tongue.

"What?"

"You have to buckle up. It saves lives. I mean, it's not like I'm planning on having an accident, but you never know. Someone could run into us and if you weren't buckled, you might be thrown through the windshield. Or if we rolled, you could be crushed under the car." She smiled. "Besides, it's the law. Haven't you seen the signs? Click it or ticket."

He groaned, but snapped the belt contraption into place.

She started the car. "Scrunch down. Remember, we don't want anyone to see you."

She gunned the car, backed into the street.

Arrth tried to duck, but the seatbelt held him upright. "This isn't working."

"That's because you have to pull the belt out to its full length before you click it. Undo it. I'll show you what I mean."

He released the catch. She leaned over to pull on his belt and the car swerved off the road.

"Ohhhh," she cried, and let go of his belt. She spun the wheel first to the left and then to the right.

The car careened over the uneven ground into the little field and pushed down a wide path of dried yellow grass in its wake. Clunk. Clunk. The car shuddered when it bounced over some hidden obstacle in deep weeds.

"Hit the brake," Arrth shouted and braced himself.

Miraculously, the car slid to a stop.

The girl was crying. "What was that? What did I hit? Did I kill something?"

Arrth jumped out. Behind the back wheels lay two broken poles. Travis's fake carved feet had been smashed into unrecognizable slivers. Grinning, he hopped back into the car.

"Nothing. You just ran over some firewood. Let's go."

51: Afternoon

One hour, forty-five minutes until device failure . . .

"THANKS for the ride." He'd had the skin-girl drop him off two driveways beyond Mick and Maria's place.

On this stretch of the highway, tall fir trees lined both sides of the road. Although the view of the river was blocked by the lush vegetation, the rush of water filtered through the trees.

His skin pricked in the cool shade.

He waited while she swung the car around in a tight turn in the middle of the road and headed back toward town. He waved, thankful he'd survived. It had been a wild ride.

Every minute counted now, so he took a shortcut through the orchard instead of following the long, winding driveway to the house.

He could see Mick's red pickup parked at the side of the house. He wondered if his dad already lay on the back. A car had tuned off the main road and was driving down the driveway. Oh, no. His heart dropped to his toes when he recognized the maroon paint. What was Meeker doing here? He would ruin everything.

Arrth ducked behind a gnarled Gravenstein apple tree and scanned the yard. An overripe apple plopped on his head. He hardly felt it.

Meeker parked in front of the house. The driver's door squeaked open, and Meeker stepped out.

It was like everything was happening in slow motion.

Mick materialized from behind the pickup and ambled towards the front of the house.

Meeker climbed the steps to the front porch.

Mick was now halfway to the front of the house.

Arrth slipped closer and hid behind Maria's flowering camellia bush. He barked like a hound dog.

Meeker jumped. His body began to twitch, and he pounded on the door.

Mick stopped and his eyes scanned the yard.

Arrth barked a second time. Louder. He waved his arms. Look this way.

Meeker used both fists and pounded harder. It sounded like he was about to break the door down.

Mick took a step forward. His eyes still searched the yard.

Arrth risked a third yip.

Mick finally spotted him. He held up his hand, palm out, and walked out front. He tiptoed up behind the fat little man and put his hand on his shoulder. "Meeker. You trying to break down my door?"

"Whoooo!" Meeker shouted in surprise. "You almost give me a heart attack. There's a dog after me."

"I don't see a dog," Mick said.

"It was here, I'm telling you. It almost bit me."

"It's gone now. What do you want?"

Meeker stood straighter and licked his lips. "I've come for the boy."

"He's still at school. The bus drops him off around four. You're welcome to wait."

"The boy isn't at school. He never showed up today."

"What!" Mick said. "He's been missing all day? Why didn't the school call?"

"They sent for me, instead," Meeker said, all puffed up with self-importance.

"But I'm his foster father. I should have been informed the minute he went missing. He could have been kidnapped."

Wow. Mick was really laying it on. Would Meeker buy it?

The truant officer pointed his finger in the air and shook it while he talked. "No. No. No. No one took him. He took himself. The boy is bad news. In less than a week, he's given me more trouble than all the children I've ever placed." He stabbed the air with his index finger. "You're going to thank me. I'm taking the boy back."

"You can't do that," Mick said. "It'd break Maria's heart."

"Better me fracturing her heart a little than that boy destroying all her hopes and dreams with his unholy shenanigans."

Mick leaned into the man's face. "I think you're overstating the situation. Art is not a bad boy. He's just a little high-spirited. You know, boys will be boys."

"So you condone his cutting school, lying, trespassing, and stealing." Meeker stepped back, pulled out a notebook, and started scribbling. "Maybe the county should reconsider placing children in a household that has no respect for the law."

"I didn't say that." Mick's voice grew taut. "Skipping school doesn't cut it in this house. Neither does lying or stealing. I promise you, when he gets home, he will be punished."

A sinister grin creased Meeker's face. "You've got that right. He will be punished. I know his kind. I'm no fool. I know what he's up to. The question is, do you?"

"I'm not sure what you're talking about," Mick said. "But if he's that bad, maybe you should take him away. I have Maria's safety to think about."

"Now you're talking sense."

"Let's search his room," Mick said. "Maybe he left a clue we can use to find him."

"Good idea."

Mick opened the front door and motioned for Meeker to enter first. "His room is upstairs, second door on the left. Go on up. I'll join you in a second. I left the water running. I'll be right back."

Mick waited a few seconds, his head cocked to one side, and then he sprang into action. In two quick strides he was off the porch and headed for Arrth. He reached into his pocket and pulled out a ring of keys.

"Take these," he said and handed Arrth the keys. "I'll keep Meeker busy upstairs while you get your dad up from the basement and into the truck."

"What if he sees us?"

"He won't. I'll make sure of that. Even if I have to stage a heart attack." He reached out, grabbed Arrth's hand, and gave it a good shake.

"But who's going to drive us to the mountain top?"

"You are."

"Me?"

"Yeah."

"But he'll see us drive away. He'll chase us."

"Not with four flat tires he won't," Mick said. "Now get going."

52: Afternoon

One hour, thirty minutes until device failure . . .

ARRTH crept down the basement stairs. It seemed dark after the bright outdoors; the air warm and stuffy. He couldn't risk turning on the light with Meeker in the house. He paused at the bottom, squeezed his eyes tight, and counted to ten. The cement floor felt cold underfoot.

When he opened his eyes, he made out the familiar shadows of the room.

The washer and dryer machines.

A table Maria used to fold and stack clean clothes.

The long blanket curtain that hung in the far corner.

"Dad!" he whisper-shouted and tiptoed across the room.

He pushed back the curtain. His father looked like a dark furry bulge dumped on the narrow cot. "Dad. It's me. Wake up."

His father didn't move.

Fear seized Arrth. He laid his ear over his father's heart. Listening.

"Nnnnnnnuuuuuk," erupted from his father's lips while he sucked in air.

Arrth jumped back.

"Whissssssssssshhhh," came the exhale.

Arrth shook his father's shoulder. "Dad. Wake up. It's time to go."

"What? What? Arrth?"

"We have to leave. Now."

His father sat up, shaking off the sleep. "Where's Tahhmic?"

"In my room -- upstairs. Meeker's with him."

"The adult skin-face who's hunting us?"

Arrth nodded.

"What's he doing here?"

"Looking for me. He's searching the house. We have to get out of here before they come back downstairs."

His father struggled to stand. Arrth grabbed his arm. "Just lean on me."

His father snorted. "The plan was for me to rescue you. Not the other way around."

"Doesn't matter who rescues who. What's important is that we get the cloaking device back in the next hour and a half." They'd crossed to the bottom of the stairs.

It took longer than expected to reach the top. Even with Arrth's help, his father had to rest every other step.

Arrth pushed open the door into the kitchen and froze.

"Looks like he was planning to run away," Meeker's voice said. He clumped down from the second floor into the kitchen. "You sure he didn't come back and take all his stuff?"

Arrth pulled the basement door closed, leaving a tiny crack to peer through. Mick and Meeker entered the kitchen.

"I've been here all morning," Mick said. "There's no way he came back and took all of his stuff with him or I would have noticed."

Meeker stood at the sink and looked out the window. "Anyplace else on the property where he may have hid his things?"

Mick glanced toward the basement. Arrth opened the door a smidgen wider. Mick's eyes widened. He gave a quick shake of his head and frowned. "Let me think. He did seem to spend a lot of time in Maria's greenhouse."

Maria's green house? What was Mick talking about? There wasn't a green house on the property; just the barn, the garage, and the little glass plant house.

"He might have stashed his stuff there," Mick said.

"Maybe we should check the basement first, while we're here."

Arrth held his breath and crossed his toes. No. No. No. Not the basement.

"He's not that stupid," Mick said.

"What do you mean?"

"If he's what you say he is, would he choose a trap with only one exit?"

Meeker mopped his brow with his white cloth and nodded. "You're right. He wouldn't. Let's check out the greenhouse."

Arrth waited until he heard the door slam and counted to sixty.

"Come on, Dad. This is our only chance."

Arrth half dragged his father across the kitchen, out the back door, down the porch steps, and to the red pickup truck. Mick had already put a mattress in the bed of the truck.

"The one thing I've learned in the last few days," Arrth said and helped his father into the back, "is that plans never go the way they're supposed to."

"What do you mean?"

"Mick can't drive us."

"WHAT!"

"We have to make our escape while he keeps Meeker occupied."

"Then how are we going to get back? I can't walk that far." His father slumped. "You'll have to go without me."

"Not a chance." Arrth pulled out the ring of keys and gave them a shake. "See these? They're the pickup keys." He grinned. "And I'm your driver."

"You can control this machine?"

"Uh-huh. Now lie down and keep absolutely still."

Arrth grabbed a bright blue tarp, covered his dad, and tucked the stiff edges of plastic tarp under the mattress. It would be a disaster if it flew off in town.

Satisfied it was secure, he jumped into the truck. Why hadn't Mick cleaned out the cab? He shoved the cloaking device next to a cardboard box of bottles in the passenger seat. On the floor were three bags of aluminum cans.

He slid the key into its slot.

RRRRRRrrrrrr. RRRRRRrrrrrr. RRRRRRrrrrr.

"Come on truck. Start!" Arrth pounded the dash.

Rrrrrmmmmm. Rrrrrrmmmmm. The engine hummed. He put it into gear and the truck rolled forward. He pushed on the gas pedal.

The pickup moved faster.

Past the house.

Past the garage.

Past the glass plant house.

Meeker came out, waving his hands. "Stop! Stop! I order you to stop."

Standing behind the truant officer, Mick waved Arrth on.

Arrth pushed the gas pedal to the floor, and the truck shot forward, spraying gravel in its wake.

53: Afternoon

One hour, ten minutes until device failure . . .

ARRTH checked the chronometer on the dash of the truck. There was just a little over an hour to get the perimeter device in place. Or . . .

"Stupid pickup truck," Arrth muttered while he wrenched the steering wheel left to avoid hitting a tall fir tree. What was wrong with the dumb machine?

Whoa! Now he was headed for a fence post. He slammed on the brakes, stopping just inches from the fence. The cloaking device slid forward and almost toppled off the seat. He grabbed it and put it on the floor.

Driving without Mick sitting next to him and telling him what to do was a disaster.

He backed up.

Why wouldn't the pickup drive in a straight path? He barely touched the wheel and the pickup took off in one direction or another. Unless he got it under control, Meeker would have all four tires fixed and catch up.

His heartbeat began to race up and down his spine.

Think. Think. Think!

Slow down.

And think.

Maybe the problem was that he was driving four times faster than during his one and only lesson. What if driving fast made the pickup turn fast? He eased up on the gas pedal and the little red needle on the speedometer dropped to the fifteen.

He turned the steering wheel a little to the right. Then, a little to the left. Both times the pickup truck did exactly what he expected.

"Wahoooo," he shouted out the window. He had it under control.

At the main road, he looked both ways. No traffic. He turned onto the pavement and headed toward town.

He was getting the hang of driving, so he speeded up. The red needle now pointed halfway between the twenty and thirty. He was cruising.

"HONK! HONK! HONK!" blasted a car horn from behind.

Arrth flinched and almost lost control.

Vibrating boom music from behind shook the leaves of the trees lining the narrow highway. He felt a pressure beat in the air and grabbed tighter onto the steering wheel.

Behind him, in the little mirror above the front window, a low-slung blue car looked like it was practically attached to the back of the pickup. It kept blaring its horn. The driver waved three fingers out the window and shouted.

Arrth rolled down his window but couldn't hear the driver's words over the roar of the engines and the music.

He slowed until the red needle pointed to the ten.

The trailing car continued to blast its horn around the next three turns. Arrth went slower and slower. He wished there was a place to pull over, to get off the road, but it was too narrow.

Up ahead, the curving road left the cover of the trees and morphed into a straight path through vegetable fields sprouting corn, tomatoes, grapes, and occasional houses.

The little blue car roared past; its driver glared and shook his fist while he rocketed by. Arrth sighed and flexed his fingers, now damp with sweat.

Before he knew it, he'd reached the straightaway approach to town. On the right sat the school. To the left loomed the gravel mountains. A white van box with flashing red lights and a siren pulled out in front of him.

He pulled off to the side of the road.

On the back of the van was the word AMBULANCE in big bold letters. It sped up the hill and disappeared at the top.

Don't panic now. All he had to do was get through town, find the logging road, and they'd be home free. But what if someone recognized him driving though town? That would ruin everything.

Mick had left a head-cover on the seat, a black and red hat with a long bill. Arrth put it on and pulled the brim down to shade his face. Under the hat had been a pair of dark eyeglasses. He put them on, too. Satisfied with his reflection in the mirror, he grinned. He wouldn't recognize himself in this disguise.

He jumped out and went to the side of the truck bed. "Dad, you okay?"

"Yeah. Are we there yet?"

"Almost. I wanted to check the tarp before we drove through town."

"Why through town? Can't we go around it?"

"No. We have to go through it to get to the quarry. From there we take the logging road up the mountain. Basically we'll be re-striding the steps you made to town."

"You're sure it's safe?"

"It's fine. Just lay still like a log."

Arrth hopped back into the cab, started the pickup, and drove back onto the road.

How odd. Near the top of the hill, three mini-fires sprouted on the edge of the pavement. When he got closer, he saw that they burned from red sticks. Fascinating. He was so busy looking at the flaming sticks that he almost rammed into the back of a car stopped in the middle of the road.

He slammed on the brakes. "Spider spit."

There wasn't just one car parked in the road, but a trail of cars. They inched forward and stopped. Arrth did the same. Again and again. Up ahead he could see three sets of red flashing lights.

On top of the ambulance.

On top of a black-and-white car.

On top of a familiar green-and-white sheriff's car.

He frowned and ground his teeth. He glanced at the chronometer. Triple worm snot! He had less than an hour.

Deputy Brown stood in the center of the pavement, his feet straddling the yellow line. He directed traffic. On the edge of the road lay the little blue car flipped up on its side. The driver sat on the ground, his head in his hands.

Arrth pulled the hat brim lower.

Don't let him recognize me.

When it was his turn to drive past the accident, he didn't dare look left or right, but he could feel Travis's father's gaze bore into him.

"You, kid. In the red Dodge. Pull over," Officer Brown shouted.

Arrth gritted his teeth and kept going.

In the mirror, he could see the man waving for him to stop. Arrth sped up.

Officer Brown sprinted to his car.

"Eeeeeeeeeee," sounded the police car's siren.

Arrth tromped on the gas. The pickup truck careened onto Highway 299.

54: Afternoon

Forty-five minutes until device failure . . .

Arrth checked the rear-view mirror.

The sheriff's car sped around the corner, its siren screaming, in pursuit.

Arrth looked back to the road ahead. He was almost to the turnoff, but if he slowed to make the turn, Deputy Brown would catch them for sure.

Think!

The box of bottles next to him on the seat rattled.

He glanced back again.

The police car was right on his tail. The siren stopped and Deputy Brown's voice came from a loudspeaker. "Stop the car. Or I will have to shoot out your tires."

Arrth wasn't stopping. Not now. Not ever.

He grabbed a bottle and flung it out the window. It bounced off the windshield of the police car. The car veered sharply to the right.

He threw another one.

And another three.

And another four.

And another six.

The box was empty, so he flung it out, too.

"Hold on, Dad," he shouted out the window and swung the wheel hard to make the turn. The pickup slid into a spin.

Officer Brown's car screeched while it swerved to miss the pickup. It flew past, just missing the back bumper, and slammed into a fire hydrant. Water gushed from under the car.

The pickup stopped its spinning and faced the road to the quarry.

Arrth glanced at the wrecked sheriff car.

Deputy Brown jumped out and started running towards the pickup. He fumbled at the gun on his belt.

Arrth stepped on the gas, and roared up the dirt road.

55: Afternoon

Twenty minutes until device failure . . .

A thick trail of dust chased behind the pickup, powdering the grass, brush, and trees in its wake. They roared through the quarry and started up the logging road.

Up ahead, a sturdy metal gate spanned the road. There was no way around it.

Arrth stopped, but left the engine running, and hopped out.

"We're at the gate," he said and pulled back the tarp.

His father sat up. "It's about time. Were you trying to kill me back there?"

Arrth laughed and helped his dad into the front seat.

He sprinted to the gate. A huge chain with a combination lock secured the gate to an anchor post. Just like Mick had said it would. No one could go through without the combination. Arrth grinned.

The combination was Mick's own private joke. Three. Six. Six. Eight. On a phone keypad it spelled F-O-O-T.

It took only minutes to swing the gate open, drive through, and lock it behind them.

"We're almost home. Want to drive?" Arrth asked.

His father snorted. "We're not into the woods yet."

"I hope not." Arrth started to laugh. "Or we'd still be in Willow Creek. Driving is pretty snarfy. Sure you don't want to give it a try?"

"No." Pause. "Arrth, I want you to know I'm proud of you. Your mother was wrong. You were ready for your *Night Out*."

"Thanks."

The road started to disappear. Limbs dipped low and scratched paint. Tiny seedlings sprouted in the wheel tracks. In another hundred years, all signs of the logging road would be gone.

When he could drive no farther, Arrth pulled to a stop. "We walk from here," he said and shut off the engine. He broke off a stout branch and handed it to his dad for a walking stick.

"Thanks. How's Tahhmic going to get his truck back?"

"Mick said he has a two-wheel machine called a motorcycle. He'll ride it up, throw it in the back, and drive back to town."

"Why do you keep calling him Mick instead of Tahhmic?"

"Because that's who he is now, and it's okay. He makes a pretty good skin-face."

"You're not thinking of."

"No. You don't have to worry," Arrth said, reading his dad's mind. "I miss my fur too much." They'd left the road and were now climbing through the trees.

His father sat on a log to rest. "Why don't you go on ahead? Once the device is in place, you can come back for me."

"Nope. Not leaving you."

"But the perimeter will fail."

"We still have ten minutes. We're almost there."

"Think of your mother."

"I am. She'd kill me if I left you." Arrth smiled. He knew he'd scored a point.

His father's eyes started to darken, and he struggled to his feet. "We're wasting time."

Minutes later they reached the clearing where it had all started. Where Arrth had pushed through the cloaked perimeter barrier. Where he'd had his first experience with a skin-face and a long gun. Where he'd picked up the granite rock and hurled it at Travis.

Five days ago that seemed like a hundred years.

His father put his hand on Arrth's shoulder. They stood side by side and stared at the unstable rocky cliff jutting skyward, knowing it hid the pathway to home.

"We're ahead of schedule," Arrth said. "We still have three minutes."

He'd barely spoken the words when they heard the distant sound of a, "Whoop, whoop, whoop." The helicopter. It was headed in their direction.

The rocky cliff dissolved and the pathway became visible. For the first time in a thousand years, someone on the outside could see into Bigfoot county.

"Hurry," his father urged and hobbled toward the path.

Arrth slung the pack off his back and pulled out the missing cloaking device.

The "WHOOP, WHOOP, WHOOP" grew louder.

His father still a few feet from the entrance.

"Quick, Dad, get inside. They have cameras."

Arrth rushed forward, set the device in place, and shoved his father.

He stared at the horizon and watched the helicopter's approach while it lifted above the tree line. He could see the pilot and the same cameraman that had been on the sandy beach with Travis. They hadn't spotted Arrth or his father yet. Did that mean the cloaking device was operational?

He put out his hand and felt for the invisible barrier. Its sting ran from the tips of his ears to the bare soles of his feet. He laughed and started jumping up and down.

"It's working!"

56: Morning

Two weeks later

Arrth stood with Uulmer just outside the cloaked perimeter. Rattles was draped around his neck.

"It looks just like new," Uulmer said. "And your idea to make mini-cloakers for the larger cloaking devices was brilliant."

Arrth smiled. "Thanks."

"So how does it feel to be a hero? That was sure some ceremony last week. You're the first younger to be knighted into The Order of the Bigfoot."

Arrth grinned.

A branch snapped. Arrth's soft brown eyes widened when the rocky slope shimmered. Was something wrong? Was the device malfunctioning? Again?

An enormous hairy foot emerged from a moss-covered boulder. A startled jackrabbit bounced into action, and Arrth grinned. Whew! He recognized the foot. It was his father's.

His dad handed Travis's mini-talker to Arrth. "This thing has been chirping for the last half hour. It's driving your mother crazy."

"You didn't have to bring it out here."

"Yes, I did. I had to get out of the cave. Your mother is driving me nuts. She decided that with everything packed up for the aborted evacuation, it would be a great time to redecorate. She's planning to tint the walls. I can only imagine what this is going to cost me. Amethyst for our pod, aquamarine for the main cave, and now that you're a hero, real rubies for your pod."

"Bachelorhood does have its perks," Uulmer said and laughed.

"I wonder who called?" Arrth flipped it open and pushed the

redial button. Travis probably wanted his phone back.

"Hello." It was Katie's voice. "Is that you, Arrth?"

"Hey."

"What are you doing?" she asked.

"Nothing much. You?"

"Mick dropped me off at the gate. I brought lunch. Peanut butter sandwiches, lasagna, pears, bananas, potato chips, and some of Maria's oatmeal cookies. You interested?"

"I'll be there in ten minutes."

"You'll be where?" his father asked. New worry lines creased his face.

"Around. Don't worry, I'll be back before dinner. Mom's fixing acorn stew. Can you take Rattles? He doesn't belong outside."

Arrth raced down the hill, slipping and sliding. He found Katie sitting on a blanket, surrounded by a feast. He plunked down next to her. It was good to see her. He'd missed her. He'd even missed school. Now that he was back, the valley seemed even more isolated.

"Hey," he said. He held out the mini-talker. "I guess you'd better give this back to Travis."

"But how will we stay in touch?"

"With this," he said and slipped a necklace over her head. A metal Bigfoot hung from its chain. "I have one, too." He held up what looked like a gold shark tooth." They work like mini-talkers, but smaller, and don't need to be recharged."

"How's it work?"

"All you have to do is push its nose and talk. When you're through, just say, hang up."

"Wow," she said. "And it's pretty cool looking, too."

"I thought you'd like it. Now tell me what happened after I left."

"Travis is on a two-month restriction because of his Bigfoot hoax. They found the gorilla suit in the tree. His dad was furious."

Arrth started stuffing cookies in his mouth. He hadn't realized until now how lonely the last two weeks had been. He wished Katie was a Bigfoot. Then he wouldn't be the only kid in the valley. "And Meeker?"

"Meeker was arrested for foster care fraud, but they couldn't find any real evidence after you disappeared so they fired him. He's washing dishes at Cinnabar Sam's."

"That's a good thing. He didn't like kids. I wonder why he took that job in the first place."

"He was just trying to impress Ms. Hammerhead."

Arrth started on a peanut butter sandwich.

"Aren't you going to ask about Tamara?"

"What about her?"

"She doesn't like you anymore. A new boy checked in last week and she's all ga-ga about him."

"Poor guy."

They both laughed.

"Oh, I almost forgot." She reached into her pack and pulled out a small cloth-wrapped bundle. She handed it to him.

"What is it?"

"I don't know. It's from Mick."

He carefully unwound the cloth. When he saw what it was, he grinned. In his hand, he held a Birchwood carving of a perfectly proportioned Bigfoot. Not just any Bigfoot. It was Arrth. Or what Arrth had looked like covered in fur.

"He said to say that friends never die, they just slowly morphify. What does that mean?"

"That friends are friends forever." He stood up. "I just had a snarfy idea. How would you like to play a little game of Skin-face and Bigfoot? You can be the Bigfoot and I'll be the skin-face."

ACKNOWLEDGEMENTS

A special thanks to my advanced readers for their valuable suggestions and advice: Jana Reveles, Christine Sackey, and Sue Wyshynski.